First edition published in 2025
ISBN/SKU: 970 1-7642625-2-1
EISBN: 978-1-7642625-3-8
Written by Salim Ibn Ahmad
Published by SleepForm Studio

Website: www.sleepformstudio.com
Email: contact@sleepformstudio.com

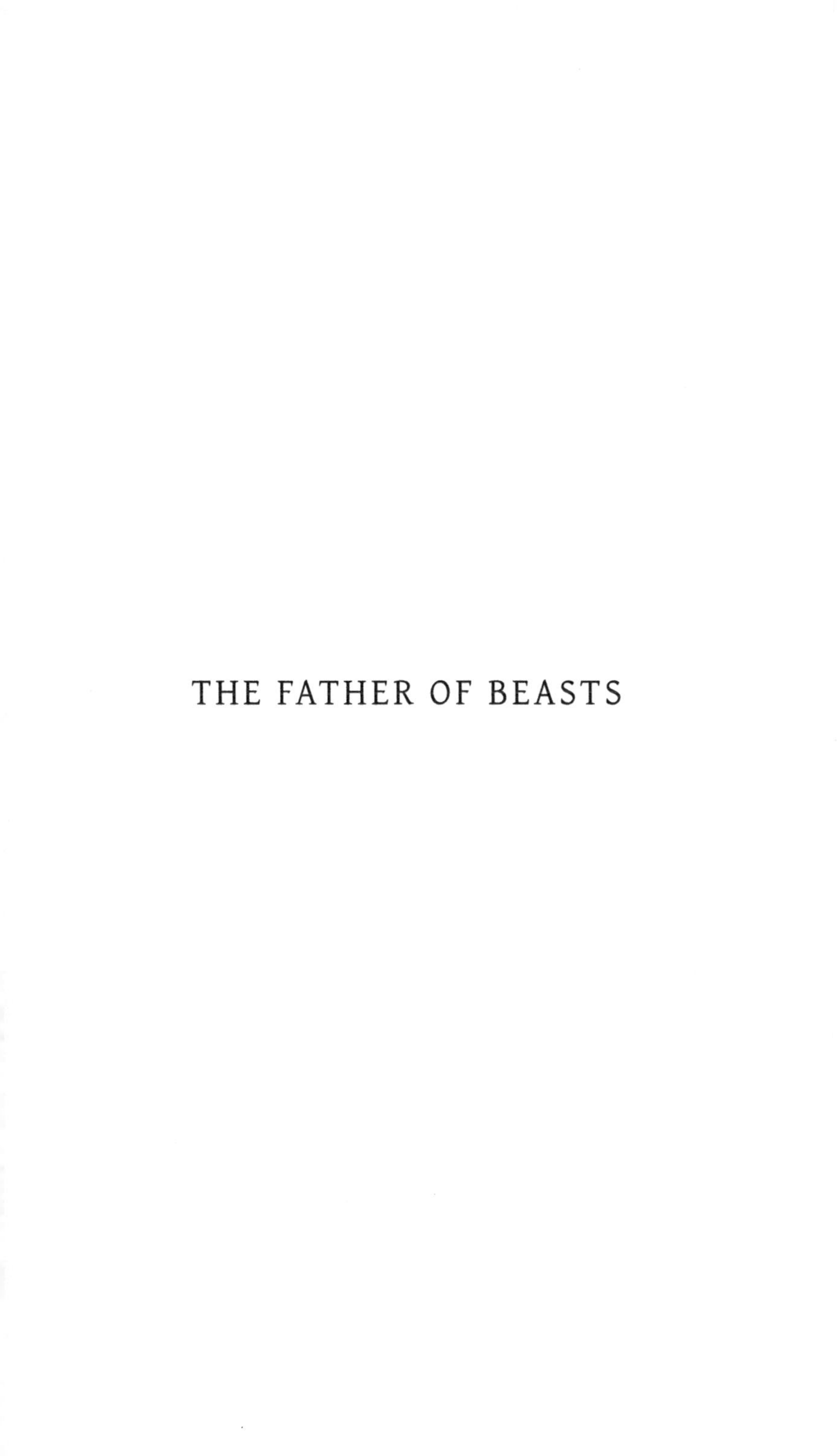

THE FATHER OF BEASTS

The Father of Beasts

SALIM IBN AHMAD

CONTENTS

~~

Chapter 1 — The Siege Tower

~~

Chapter 2 — The Crush

~~

Chapter 3 — The Demon Awakens

~~

DISCLAIMER

This book is built upon real history. It follows the chronicles of the First Crusade; only its characters are imagined. It seeks to honour truth, not senseless violence.

I was unaware of the history of the First Crusade before I started imagining a story set during this time, once I learned it, I was compelled to write about it. Every city, march, atrocity and siege is drawn from the chronicles of Muslim and Frankish writers of the Crusades, these were not inventions. The massacres and rivers of blood were real.

Ahmad — the so-called Father of Beasts— is fiction. His beasts, his Brotherhood — imagined. But the struggle he embodies is not, he is based off of a combination of Muslim historical figures and narrations. His life is a lens, a realistic way to walk the roads of the Holy Land (Bilad al-Sham) in 1098–1099 and see events as they unfolded. He stands for those whose names were never written, though they bore the weight of history.

The purpose of this work is not to change history, but to remember it through the eyes of one man who could have existed there — to walk beside him, and not to forget.

OPENING DEDICATION

For those slaughtered by the cruelty of power.
For those erased by the silence of history.
For those who endured when the world preferred that they had broken.

OPENING AUTHOR'S NOTE

I write of true men, and of the cowards who stood in their way.

I write of the innocent who were torn down and betrayed, of a time of weakness and selfishness not unlike our own.

I write so that knowledge and memory be not buried beneath the lies of the powerful.

I write with hope — that men may stand again as they once did, in a time now gone. I write and I pray — that the worst may yet be stopped from repeating itself in the coming years.

This is not just a story, but the cycle of truth and falsehood. It is the echo of the past, warning the present.

I open with the words of Allah:

"Among the believers are men true to what they promised Allah. Among them is he who has fulfilled his vow [to the death], and among them is he who awaits [his chance]. And they did not alter [the terms of their commitment] by any alteration"

— Quran 33:23

EPIGRAPHS

"If you had been there, your feet would have been stained to the ankles with the blood of the slain. It was a just and splendid judgement of God that this place should be filled with the blood of unbelievers."
— Raymond of Aguilers, chaplain of the First Crusade (1099)

"The Franks came out to your land, and like a raging torrent they poured across the land, destroying, pillaging, slaughtering, and enslaving."
— Abū'l-Muẓaffar al-Abiwardi, elegy after the fall of Jerusalem (c. 1100–1101)

PREFACE

In 1095, Pope Urban II called the warriors of Christendom to march east. Tens of thousands answered. They crossed mountains and rivers with one vow on their lips — to free Jerusalem.

By 1098, Antioch had fallen after a bitter siege. The Franks were starving, fever-ridden, half-mad with zeal — yet still they pressed south. Their next prey was not a fortress of kings but a small Syrian city: Ma'arrat al-Nu'man. Behind its walls waited no army, only farmers, hunters, and children.

But the Franks were not alone in their cruelty. The Muslim world was divided, its rulers no less guilty. Seljuks and Fatimids fought each other while their people starved. Bayt al-Maqdis (Jerusalem) changed hands like a coin tossed on a table. To kings and amirs (leaders) alike, cities were wagers, and the currency was the blood of the poor.

This was the real war: not only armies in the field, but betrayals in the halls of power. While peasants sowed and children begged, those in authority bargained away their homes. While prayers rose from mosques and churches, rulers weighed lives against crowns. Every banner, every oath, was stained with contempt for those they claimed to protect.

So when the Franks turned south, Jerusalem was already broken — by hunger, by siege, and by the selfishness of its own lords.

What happened at Ma'arra would echo across centuries — not in glory, not in victory, but in hunger, cruelty, and the shadow of fear that men carried into the Holy Land.

And from the ashes of Ma'arra, one figure would rise.

CHAPTER 1 — THE SIEGE TOWER

The city had run out of bread before it ran out of breath. For two weeks Ma'arra had held. By day, smoke ringed the sky. By night, the clouds glowed red. They were not soldiers on the walls—just farmers with rope burns across their palms, masons with lime under their nails, boys clutching slings, old men who had once hunted boar in the hills.

And among them stood the one everyone watched from the corner of their eyes: Ahmad, the town's Abu al-Wuhush (Father of Beasts).

He looked carved out of the hills themselves. Long black hair hung loose around a heavy beard. Scars lined his forearms. His shoulders were broad, his step steady, every movement deliberate. When he lifted his bow, the noise along the parapet thinned to silence.

A wolf stayed at his heel — Nahhas, blue-eyed, scar-muzzled, black coat, raised from a pup torn orphan in the hills and hasn't left his side since. Above, the hawk Reeh circled, once a starving fledgling he nursed back to health, now his shadow in the sky. In the gate-tower, Adham hammered iron hooves, his father's black stallion and his only inheritance, scarred but unbroken. His family.

Across the plain, the siege tower rolled closer. Raw timbers bound with iron, hides soaked in water to drink fire. It loomed taller than the wall by a man's height. Oxen strained at the yokes in its shadow. Ropes stretched tight as men dragged, chanting low and steady. Mantlets crawled with it like beetles, shields of thick planks inching toward the ditch. Behind the hides were iron-capped men in white, red crosses chalked across their tunics.

Beyond the tower, banners marked who had brought this storm. Ahmad did not know their words, but he knew the gesture when a hand lifted and men moved forward to kill.

"Why us?" a woman asked, clutching a wrapped infant. "We are farmers. We have no coin."

Another man spat dark phlegm. "They promised mercy if we opened the gates. Lies. The Franks keep no oaths."

A boy with a sling muttered, "There is no army here."

Ahmad gave no answer. He simply drew and loosed.

His first arrow caught a torch-bearer at a range most men guessed at. Fire and man dropped together. His second shaft punched through a mantlet plank and dropped the soldier hiding behind. A third arrow flew through the narrow V where two boards met, buried in a throat. A helmet lifted above a shield for a look; Ahmad put an arrow straight through the visor hinge.

Four arrows. Four bodies. The murmuring on the wall stopped cold.

"Wall!" someone shouted. Stones and arrows rained down, clattering harmlessly against wet hides. Ahmad saved his shafts. He slowed his breathing, fingers smoothing the yew as if calming a horse. Above him, Reeh screeched. Nahhas pressed against Ahmad's leg, silent, scar muzzle twitching.

"Keep your tongues steady," the mason barked, but his eyes still flicked toward Ahmad, looking for strength.

The tower crept another cart-length forward. Water still seeped from its hides. At its base, teams strained, curses rising. Men shoved mattocks under wheels stuck in the churned mud. Beyond them, iron glinted like a field of stars. The ram pounded at the lower gate, dull and heavy, stone groaning with each strike.

"Allah (God) have mercy," the woman with the child whispered. "Why do they come with prayers on their mouths and iron in their hands?"

Ahmad listened to the chant rolling from the plain, harsh and guttural. He didn't know the tongue, but he remembered the sounds.

"They come because they think the world is theirs," the mason answered.

Ahmad searched for the one the others followed—the baton-holder, the heartbeat of the push. At this distance, most men would waste arrows. Ahmad breathed out slow, let the wind tell his fingers what to do, and loosed.

The baton fell. The ropes lost rhythm. For a dozen heartbeats the tower faltered.

On the wall, men whispered thanks under their breath.

Others fired at whatever they could see, arrows clattering off hides. Ahmad picked only the openings: a calf behind a shield, a throat stretched in a yell, a hand too long on a torch. His arrows cut work, not air.

"No one shoots like him," the mason muttered.

A sling-stone sparked against the merlon by Ahmad's head. Nahhas didn't flinch. The wolf leaned harder into him, steady as stone. A few braver men touched the animal's back for luck, then pulled away quickly.

Down the line, boys flung pebbles. Men dragged up jars of water, the last scraps of pitch. A crooked chain of hands passed stones up to the crenels. The air filled with ash, burned hide, sweat.

"Their songs," the woman said, her face pale. "They sing like they pray."

"They do," the mason told her. "Pray to win, same as us."

"And if we don't?"

"Then we bury our dead and remember."

Ahmad loosed again, cutting down a crossbowman who thought himself hidden. The enemy's weapon kicked skyward as its owner fell. A cheer rose thinly. Ahmad didn't look up—his quiver was light. His fingers found each shaft by feel, knowing its balance, its weight, like bones of his own.

"Father of Beasts," whispered one sling-boy, awe mixed with fear. "They say you fought a lion and came back laughing. Is it true?"

Ahmad's next arrow cracked into a shield-rim, snapping the hand behind it. "I fought what came up the path to eat goats."

"And you won?"

"Once," he said, loosing again.

The ram thudded. The tower crawled. The ditch between filled with wreckage. Breath steamed in the chill, then caught and froze. Reeh wheeled higher, her shadow brushing the tower's skin.

"Why don't they leave us be?" the woman asked.

"They want the road south," the mason said. "And pride to say they took it."

A voice farther down the line cried out: "They knew! Someone led them here!"

Another spat: "Curse the ones who sold us out."

Ahmad heard it. Even above the ram, even above the chants. He locked it in his chest like an arrow waiting on the string. There were always traitors.

His last shaft punched a torch from a hand that thought itself safe. He slung his bow and drew a short spear. The men beside him mirrored him without thinking: arrows while you had them, iron when you didn't.

Nahhas's hackles rose stiff. Ahmad touched the wolf's neck once. The fur was soot-black under his hand. Nothing more needed saying.

Reeh shrieked, rising higher. Behind them, Adham's hooves thundered against stone.

The tower came on. Its wheels found rhythm again. Ropes thrummed. Ladders rose, pawing the sky. Chants thickened. Wet hides quivered under arrow strikes, shedding them like rain.

"God will open a door," the mason muttered—he'd said it every day.

"Until He does," Ahmad rasped through smoke, "we hold."

He planted his feet. Men to his left and right followed suit. Hands tightened on spear-shafts, on stones. Below, the gate groaned.

The tower's shadow swallowed them.

"Ready!" someone cried. It might have been Ahmad. It might have been anyone.

The siege tower loomed until it filled the world—wet hide, iron pins, the breath of men who had marched across the earth to kill. A ladder clawed at the stone. The chant from the plain sharpened like teeth.

The tower lurched its final step, more fall than stride.

It had not yet kissed the parapet, but everyone knew it would in the next breath.

CHAPTER 2 — THE CRUSH

The tower leaned against the wall like a giant pushing with its shoulder. Hooks bit into stone. Wet hides rasped against the merlons. Ladders scraped and clawed until their claws caught.

Ahmad had no arrows left.

He let the bow hang at his side and gripped his short spear. Around him, townsmen stacked stones knee-high, an axe-head tied to a broom handle, pots of water set where oil should have been. Smoke thickened the air until every breath burned.

"Hold!" someone shouted. The word belonged to all of them now.

The first Frank hauled himself over the lip of the parapet, hook in hand. Ahmad stepped forward, caught the shaft under his arm, twisted, and hurled the man down between tower and wall. Another climbed up from a ladder. Ahmad drove the spear under his shield, felt ribs give, wrenched the weapon free, and stepped aside. Nahhas slammed into the next man's knee, teeth tearing.

The Frank fell sideways, and the spear meant for Ahmad struck his fellow instead.

Reeh dropped from the smoke. His talons raked across a man's cheek before he shot back into the sky. The man screamed, clutched his face, and toppled. Others flinched, raising shields against a bird they could not follow.

"Push them off!" the mason cried. For a while, the men near him did. Wood and iron met bodies. The tower spilled men onto the stones. The first wave died under clubs and spears; the second walked on their corpses. Long spears stabbed over shields. Hooks caught belts and wrists and dragged defenders down. Steel went to work where it was strongest—up close.

Ahmad snapped a spear shaft with his forearm and struck back without pause. He saw not faces but targets—an elbow, a groin, a throat turned wrong under a helm. He fought like a hunter when the boar turns, every move meant to end. Around him, townsmen steadied themselves to his rhythm without knowing it. For a time, the wall held.

Then the ram at the lower gate boomed. The stone gave a tired groan, promising to break soon.

The crush thickened. A man in a white tunic with a red cross climbed over the wall and swung his sword down with certainty. Ahmad met it on the spear's shaft, stepped inside, and smashed his fist into the man's mouth. Teeth broke. The sword dropped. Ahmad took it without looking at him. He tested its balance once across a shield and set himself.

Voices rose in the enemy's tongue. A chant spread: "Deus vult!" The cry rolled up ladders and through the tower, harsh and ugly.

"Back!" someone cried. "Back to the stair!" But there was no back. The men who had room to yield did; the rest went down and were trampled. White tunics pressed forward. The smell changed—more blood.

Nahhas vanished into a knot of legs and came out with his muzzle slick. He waited, watching ankles. When a man stumbled, the wolf tore his tendon and left him to the tide.

A stone the size of a man's head smashed against the wall. The parapet shook under Ahmad's boots. Another stone hit higher, tearing away a merlon and the walkway under it. Men fell with the stone. The wall line broke and spilled like water from a jar.

Ahmad went with them.

The fall wasn't far, but it was onto stone. He landed on hip, shoulder, then head. The shock tore the air out of him. The sword slid away, then his hand found it again and locked on as if it were a branch in a river.

Bodies crashed after him. One landed across his ribs, another pinned his arm, another pressed down on his legs. Pain flared, then dulled. He tried to roll but couldn't. Boots trampled the pile—friend and enemy alike. A shield rim rang against the stone by his head. Screams cut close. A groan went low as steel went in.

Above him, through the gap in the broken parapet, he saw a strip of sky the colour of tarnished copper. The tower loomed through smoke. Faces appeared, vanished, replaced by more. Some voices cried "Christe!" Others shouted nothing, just worked like men in a slaughterhouse.

Nahhas growled close—low, guttural, teeth in flesh—then his sound was swallowed by the noise. Reeh crossed the strip of sky once, a blur against smoke, and vanished.

Ahmad's mouth filled with blood from the fall and the weight pressing him. He tried to spit but couldn't turn. The blood slid back into his throat. His chest rattled. Still his hand gripped the sword. He couldn't lift it, but he would not let it go.

The world shrank to touch: cold stone under his back; a belt buckle grinding into his ribs; the tick of another man's blood running down his arm; grit under his teeth. The stink changed again—burned pitch, hair, excrement, something sickly sweet.

Far in the city a woman called for a child. Nearer still, a child cried for its mother. The ram hit the gate again. Stone groaned. One more blow would do it.

Ahmad forced his breaths small, like a man under a river counting heartbeats. Boots struck stone near his ear. A spear probed the pile, hit bone, and rang like a stick on a pot.

"Avance!" someone shouted in the enemy tongue. The weight shifted. For a moment Ahmad thought he might be dragged free, but more bodies fell and crushed him flatter. His vision went to sparks, then black, then back again to that strip of sky.

He remembered how these same voices had once promised mercy before knives. Now the mouths shouted prayers as swords cut flesh.

He held the sword like a prayer, even if he could not lift it.

Another part of the parapet gave way. Dust rose. Men on the tower cheered. On the ground, men only groaned. The chant swelled again: "Deus! Christe!".

His head hammered. The strip of sky turned dark. Smoke filled it. The weight on him pressed like stone.

He tried again to move his arm. Couldn't. The pommel dug into his palm. He thought of Adham stamping in the gate-tower, Reeh's shadow falling across men's eyes, Nahhas with teeth sunk deep. He did not think of anything else.

Above, a white hem stained brown moved in the smoke. A man with a cross stepped where others had fallen. Another in a wool cap looked down, then turned away.

The ram struck again. The gate answered.

The strip of sky narrowed.

He drew what little air he could find and kept it. He passed out, it wasn't like a blow but slow and certain.

And he did not wake again until night.

CHAPTER 3 — THE DEMON AWAKENS

Night woke him. Cold tightened on his skin, turning sweat into a shiver. Weight pinned his ribs and thigh. His right hand ached. When he tried to open it, he found he had clamped a foreign sword so tightly the studs in the hilt had stamped their shape into his palm.

Smoke rolled low across the stones, thick with pitch and fat. The strip of sky he had last seen was gone. Above him glowed only red fire behind the smoke.

Boots scraped close by. Voices followed — harsh, drunk, careless. Not words of the market. Torches bobbed through the wreckage, light coming and going like a man's breath.

A spear jabbed down into a body two corpses over, then again. Each time came the dull sound of iron punching what was once flesh. A torch bent lower, tracing across shields and broken men until it found Ahmad's face.

The man holding it gasped. The torch dipped. "Diable," he stammered. Louder, voice cracking: "Diable!"

Ahmad didn't know the word, but he knew its weight. The same as those other shouts on the wall — Deus, Christe. Words that cut instead of spared.

The others looked up just as Ahmad heaved.

He shoved the dead from his chest and stood. The sword came with him because his hand would not let go. His eyes were only eyes, but the men saw more than a man. One dropped his blade before he could lift it. Ahmad stepped in and drove the point up under his jaw. The sound ended before the cry left his throat. Hot blood ran across Ahmad's wrist.

"Stand," Ahmad rasped. The word was torn by smoke and blood, but to the Franks it was only noise.

The torch-bearer panicked and hurled the light at him. Oil caught splinters and rags, fire spreading across the stones in a crawling sheet. Another man thrust carefully with a spear, steady as practice.

Nahhas burst from the dark, jaws clamping the man's knee. The scream was high and short. The spear dropped. Ahmad snatched it, flipped it, and pinned the man's shoulder to the ground.

Reeh fell from the smoke, talons raking the torch-bearer's face. The man shrieked, clawing at his own eyes, and staggered away. The one with the ruined leg crawled after, leaving a red trail.

"Diable," another spat as they fled. "Il marche avec des bêtes."

By morning, the story would be simpler — and worse.

Ahmad stood. The ground tilted, then steadied. His skull hammered. He forced shallow breaths until the blood in his throat shifted and let him breathe. The sword dragged heavier now, in his arm and in his mind. He stepped out of the pile of bodies.

Ma'arra burned. Fire licked its alleys as if it had always known them. Doors stood open, houses spilling silence.

He passed a table where a cracked bowl held blackened bones, split and boiled. Flies worked a strip of meat on a plate. In another lane, a woman lay on her back, dress torn, fingers twisted in her own hair. Ahmad pulled down a burned curtain and covered her. Further on, a child's body lay face-first into a wall. He stood over it a moment before forcing himself to move.

At the slope to the fields, a column of prisoners shuffled south under guard. Rope bound them in groups. A child whimpered, hushed by her mother. Franks followed behind, swords loose at their sides.

Ahmad's leg trembled. His breath tore. Even whole, he could not have reached them. He said nothing. To cry out would only give the night his voice.

Watching the captives stumble, Ahmad felt that sight cut like a blade.

His lip curled. "Where were the men who swore to defend Ma'arra, then fled? Where were those who guided the Franks for coin? They feasted while their brothers bled. They bargained while our daughters screamed. Their silver is the blood of the helpless."

He raised his eyes to the smoke-choked sky. "Allah, strip them of honour if they will not fight for their own. If I ever stand before them, let them see what I will do to them."

His voice dropped. "O Allah, have mercy on the dead. Give me strength for the living. I will not rest while my people are in chains."

He moved deeper into the ruins. Nahhas padded ahead, ears pricked. Reeh circled above, a fleck against the glow. Twice he passed homes turned into kitchens of horror — meat roasting where children once slept. Once he saw a knuckle bone on a plate like a plum stone. He refused to name it. Names gave things weight, and this was already too heavy.

At the gate-tower, stalls lay buried under ash. A broken yoke leaned in the rubble. A shape shifted in shadow.

"Adham," Ahmad said.

The horse stepped out, soot dulling his black coat, eyes bright. He pressed his head into Ahmad's chest, steady as a heartbeat. Ahmad pressed his forehead to the stallion's, and the world steadied a little.

He slid the sword under the saddle strap, his hand unable to close properly. He mounted with effort, breath ragged.

Nahhas leapt to his side. Reeh swept low once, then climbed.

They left not by the gate but by a narrow break in the wall. The horse pushed through smoke into the fields, ash falling like frost. Behind them, Ma'arra groaned under fire.

The road of captives was empty now. Frost hardened the stubble. Ahmad let his hand sink into Nahhas's fur for warmth.

He had no far thoughts left. Only this: he would not pass chains and call it wisdom. He would not lose his name to the smoke of this night.

The horse walked on. The world slid between waking and dark. Reeh's cry thinned and vanished, then came again from another angle.

Adham carried him from the burning city, with Nahhas pressed to the stirrup and Reeh circling high, all three moving into the pale of morning while Ahmad's head fell to Adham's mane and his hands hung slack on the horse's neck.

EPIGRAPHS

"The Franks entered Ma'arra and massacred its people for three days. They killed more than one hundred thousand, and then they stayed in the town, eating human flesh."
— *Ibn al-Athīr, al-Kāmil fī al-Tārīkh*

"In Ma'arra our troops boiled pagan adults in cooking-pots; they impaled children on spits and devoured them grilled."
— *Radulph of Caen, Gesta Tancredi*

CHAPTER 4 — WHISPERS ON THE EDGE OF FIELDS

Ahmad didn't ride so much as cling to the horse while Adham chose the way. The stallion kept his steps sure and slow, carrying his master with a patience that came from long years together. Ahmad's hands barely held on. When his head dipped, Adham shifted to keep him steady.

The world reached Ahmad in fragments. Smoke in his throat. The sour stench of burned grain. The clean bite of frost over stubble. He told himself only one thing: forward.

Nahhas trotted close to the stirrup, brushing against the leather, steadying the horse with his presence. Every so often the wolf nudged Adham's belly as if to remind him: keep him safe, keep him alive. Above, Reeh circled against the paling sky, riding faint air currents, always near.

Fields stretched around them, broken by walls and the bare bones of fig trees. A stream gave itself away first by its sound, then by a silver gleam on stones. Adham waded in, pawed once, and drank deep.

After a short time, he tried to tell the horse "Forward," but the word caught and died. His skull throbbed like a struck bell.

Dawn came. Behind him, out of sight, Ma'arra was a dark bruise against the horizon. Ahead, the ordinary world still existed: thorn and dust, spider webs strung with dew, goat pellets scattered on the earth. Life that had survived the night. It felt wrong, almost indecent, that it had.

Ahmad meant to ride farther, to find shelter, to let the fever leave him. But the body has its own will. Somewhere between one stride and the next, his grip loosened. His cheek dropped onto Adham's mane, then slid. The stallion stopped, bent his knees carefully, and let his master down as gently as a pot being lowered to the ground.

Nahhas stood over him at once, body braced, ears up, eyes sweeping the field. Reeh swept low, checked, and settled on the horse's tack, feathers ruffled but watching.

That was how the villagers found him.

Shepherds were already in the fields at first light. Boys with firewood, women at the ovens, men pushing goats toward pasture. Bells jingled faintly. Then they froze, their rhythm broken, when they saw the black horse with a fallen man at its feet and a wolf guarding him.

"Back," a woman said sharply, pulling a child behind her. Dogs that had been lazy by the walls scrambled up, barked, then shrank away, sensing what stood before them.

On a rise, an older man shaded his eyes. His back was bent from a life of labour. He studied the horse, the bird, the wolf — and the man on the ground. "Be still," he told the others. "Look first."

They looked. The stallion stood without tether. The hawk perched calm, as if it had always belonged there. The wolf's gaze passed from one villager to another, then back to the fallen man, as if counting every breath between them.

"It is him," the old man said at last. "Father of Beasts."

The name passed among them like a secret. Some had heard he had fought lions in the hills, or taken down a mountain bear. Others said he spoke to strays until they followed him.

"Mind the wolf," someone muttered. Still, they came down the slope, slow and careful, staves low, palms open. Nahhas bared his teeth once — not a challenge, but a warning. The old man knelt first, lowering himself cautiously.

"Peace on you, hunter," he said. He offered the back of his hand for the wolf to scent. Nahhas sniffed, sneezed, and ignored him. That was enough.

Together they lifted Ahmad, careful as if they carried a man they'd be judged for dropping. He was lighter than he looked. They laid him on a mat in the shade of a goat-hair tent. Nahhas lay across his legs; Reeh claimed the lintel and did not move.

They brought water, wrung cloth until the bowl turned pink, loosened his belts, freed his breath. Old hands checked his nails, young ones brought goat's milk, setting it down within reach. By afternoon his fever broke into sweat, and he fell into a deep, heavy sleep.

Outside, life pressed on. Grain ground into meal. Nets were mended. Water poured into jars. Men spoke in low voices.

"They burned Ma'arra. I saw the sky from the ridge."
"Do we run to Hama? Or hide here?"
"They promised safe passage. Then butchered those who trusted them. Mercy is bait in their mouths."

Heads nodded. Ahmad did not stir, but the words cut into him all the same.

"What of Aleppo? Damascus?" another man muttered. "Their amirs (leaders) sit safe behind their walls. Do you think Ridwan will come? Do you think Duqaq will ride out?" Silence answered.

That night, Ahmad opened his eyes to steady lamplight. Wood smoke, wool, goat's milk, onions. The ordinary smells of the living. A woman noticed, gave a soft cry, and others gathered. They did not crowd him. In villages that see death often, people learn how to give space.

"You are among your people," the elder said. "Allah brought you out."

In half-sleep, Ahmad muttered. Even in dreams he heard the cries of the Franks — "Deus vult, Christe". He did not know the meaning yet, but the sound clung to him like smoke.

Ahmad managed a rough "My thanks." Nahhas pressed his head into his hand. The wolf's warmth steadied him. A woman lifted a cup to his lips; he drank, and it eased his throat. Warm bread came next, and he broke the first strip for Reeh, who took it without sound.

"Tell us of Ma'arra," a man asked quietly. "We hear... there was eating."

Ahmad said nothing. His silence was enough. They understood.

From the shadows of the tent, one of the villagers spat into the dirt.

"It wasn't only the Franks who broke us," he said bitterly. "There were men of our own who turned away. Promises of help that never came. Bread and water sold to the enemy while our children starved. We all know who."

Another nodded, voice low but steady. "Cowards with authority, safe behind walls, while Ma'arra burned."

The air in the tent grew heavier. No names were spoken, but every man and woman there seemed to hear them just the same.

Ahmad did not smile, but his gaze swept across them.

A woman wept soundlessly. The elder covered his face and whispered, "Allah is sufficient for us, and He is the best Disposer of affairs."

That night, they spoke around him while he slept. They shared stories they'd heard — of the lion in the wadi, the bear in the orchards, the wolf that walked at his side. Not to boast, but to hold onto hope.

By morning, stiffness had set in but his strength returned. He stood slowly, buckled a borrowed cloak, and slid his lion-hide hawk glove over his left hand. Its worn leather steadied him more than water had.

The elder waited at the doorway. "There is food."
"Others will need it more," Ahmad said. He checked his bowstring, then whistled Reeh down to his glove. Nahhas rose and stretched, ready.

Outside, the village gathered. Ahmad spoke short and sharp:
"Hide your grain in two places — one that can be found, one that can't. Move your women and children at night, not by the road. Do not trust the people of the cross and their broken promises. If they come, shut your gates. If they take one hostage, they'll take ten. Fight only where the ground makes a man stumble — in lanes, between walls. Save arrows. Stones on slings work just as well."

The words carried weight. The old man nodded once.
"Will you go to the amir?" someone asked.
"No, I will go where I can help," Ahmad said.
He added only: "You fed me. May Allah reward you."

He raised his hands briefly. "Allah, keep their homes hidden from the enemy, and turn harm from their doors."

They brought Adham forward, brushed free of soot. The stallion pressed his head against Ahmad's chest and blew a long breath, checking his master's strength. Ahmad leaned his forehead to the horse's, a moment of quiet before the road called again.

CHAPTER 5 — THE RAID OF THE RED CROSSES

He saddled Adham, the black stallion swiftly. The wolf, Nahhas, stood close by, and the hawk, Reeh, shifted restlessly after landing on his glove.

A shepherd came running down the slope, breath steaming in the dawn.

"They took women," he gasped. "South track, past the tamarisks. Six of them, with red crosses on their tunics. Drinking, laughing. They camped in the dry riverbed."

Ahmad's hand froze on the strap. "How long ago?"

"Before dawn. They tied the women in twos."

Ahmad nodded once. He tightened the girth. "Stay here. If you hear shouting, don't come."

Reeh lifted into the pale sky. He took off at such a speed, as if flying on his horse. Nahhas moved at Adham's side, silent, ready.

They went at a hunter's pace through scrub and thorn, down a dry channel where hooves left no dust. Ahmad read the ground as he went: dragged ropes, bootscuffs, the rim of a shield pressed into sand. He smelled wine before he saw it spilled black in the dust.

He stopped at the ridge. Below, in the hollow of the riverbed, the Franks were camped by a fire. Six men, careless. Their tunics were stained, their crosses roughly stitched. One wore mail half-laced. Two sat with shields dropped. One leaned against a spear. The women lay bound, ankles and wrists tied together by a single rope. One stared at nothing, one rocked and muttered, one watched the men with a hawk's eyes.

Two Franks made a show of keeping watch. One poked the fire with a stick. The other swayed with a wine skin, head back, laughing at nothing.

Ahmad sent Reeh high with a flick of his hand. Then he slid from the saddle, touched Nahhas' ruff, and moved down into the cover of tamarisk. He crawled until he could smell meat in the pan and hear the wine gurgle. The sword lay along his arm, its blade wrapped in cloth to kill the shine.

He whistled once, low and sharp.

Reeh dropped like a stone. Her talons raked the face of the wine skin guard. The man screamed, clutching his eyes. The other turned to shout—Ahmad slid from the shadows and cut his throat. The body fell into the fire, spilling embers.

The camp erupted. One man lunged for a knife, another for a spear. Nahhas hit the spear man at the calf, teeth locking to the bone. The man howled and fell. Ahmad stepped past him and drove his sword into the one with the knife. Blood spattered the fire.

A third Frank came up with a hatchet. Ahmad blocked the swing on his forearm, shoved in close, and stabbed twice—belly, then throat. The man dropped where he stood.

"Help us!" a woman cried in Arabic.

"I am," Ahmad said.

Another Frank, quick with his mail still half-done, rushed at him. Ahmad struck low, cutting his knee. He collapsed screaming. Reeh raked his face and he threw the shield over his head like a child hiding from rain. Ahmad ended him with one stroke.

The nasal-helmed Frank tried to kick Nahhas. He over-balanced. Ahmad's sword caught him as he fell.

The wine skin guard staggered away, blood in his eyes, trying to run. Ahmad snatched the dropped hatchet and threw. It hit square in the back. The man spun and crashed into the dust.

Then silence. Only the fire crackled, and Nahhas' growl faded as he released the calf he had ruined.

Ahmad moved to the women. The rope binding them was one long cord. He cut each knot clean, slow, careful. One woman flinched at his touch. He showed her the knife in his palm. "Here. You're free."

The oldest one among them, pointed at the fire. "They boiled—" She stopped. Another whispered, "They ate our dead. And before that..." Her voice broke. "They defiled us."

"I know," Ahmad said, his face set. "I was in Ma'arra."

They looked at him then as if he had walked out of the nightmare itself. One woman wouldn't stop weeping, another stared at the wolf sitting calm then at the hawk on its perch in amazement.

"We must move," Ahmad said. He pointed to the ridge. "Go there. The ground will hide your sound. Travel slow. Drink from the shaded spring, not the open pool." He poured water into a shallow cup and held it while the oldest drank first.

She then caught his sleeve. "Who are you?" she asked. "Are you a jinn?"

"Only a hunter," Ahmad said. "Go."

He cut strips from dead men's cloaks to bind their ankles. He gave them knives and showed them how to slash, not stab. He told them where to find shepherds by dusk, and what words to use so they would be believed.

When they were gone, he turned back to the dead. He dragged them into place around the fire. He propped shields in a circle, crosses facing up. He hung one cross-marked tunic high in a tamarisk, where the wind would shift it. He scored the sand with claw-marks from a hook of bone, so the ground looked cursed. He crumbled black ash over the red crosses until they looked stained by fire.

Reeh clicked from the shield rim. Nahhas watched, head tilted.

When the women reached the ridge, they turned once. He lifted his hand and pointed them onward.

Ahmad gathered what he could use: two knives, rope, a bowstring knotted into a sling, stale bread, salt. He found a small wooden cross near a dead man's hand. He set it back on the chest and left it where it could be seen.

"Let them fear," he said quietly.

He whistled. Reeh came to his fist. Nahhas padded to his heel. He climbed out of the riverbed. On the ridge he stopped and looked south. Dust hung far on the horizon. A great host was moving.

He touched the earth. "O Allah, guide me to those I can save."

Adham blew hard through his nose. Ahmad mounted, set the hawk loose to circle, and rode at an easy pace along the ridge.

By noon the women would be safe among shepherds. By evening the fear-scene in the wadi would be found. By dawn the story would spread: of a man with a hawk and a wolf who turned crosses into omens.

Ahmad did not look back. He rode south, toward the road where the banners of the enemy would soon stand still before another city's walls.

EPIGRAPHS

"Among the greatest of calamities were not the Franks, but those among us who betrayed their brothers, opening the way for slaughter and fire."
— Ibn al-Athīr, al-Kāmil fī al-Tārīkh (c. 1200)

"We trusted in men who promised guidance through that land, yet they turned against their own, selling us bread, water, and the keys to the villages. Such allies are more dangerous than the enemy before us."
— Albert of Aachen, Historia Ierosolimitana (early 12th century)

CHAPTER 6 — THE TRAITOR'S PRICE

Ahmad did not have to search far. He took the shepherds' path at dawn, keeping off the road. The air was cold and thin. Adham climbed steady, hooves sure on the terraces. Nahhas ranged ahead, slipping in and out of sight, and Reeh flickered above the slope, sharp against the pale sky.

The men in the goat-hair tent had given him more than bread. They had given him whispers. Not names—never names—but enough. A man from the weigh-house. A man with lime scars on his wrist. A man who showed the Franks the hidden springs. A man who led them past the guards for bread and coin.

By mid morning he saw the village. Mud walls, a small square, palm trees rising like spears. Every yard carried ruin—broken jars, broken tools, the weary look of people who slept with shoes on. He circled first, reading the land like a hunter.

He tied Adham in the shade and touched the stallion's neck. "Guard."

Nahhas crouched low, ears flat, eyes fixed. Reeh came to his glove, then lifted away at his whisper.

Ahmad walked in slow. He wanted the village to see him.

Children spotted him first. A boy pointed at the wolf until his mother grabbed his wrist. Men on a bench stopped talking. A woman pulled bread from her oven and didn't put the next in. Even the donkey brayed once, then went quiet.

Ahmad stopped where all could see him. His voice carried:

"I'm looking for a man. Scar on his wrist. He showed the Franks the hidden water. He led them by night."

The square went silent.

An old man wet his lips. "Why do you ask?"

"Because Ma'arra burned," Ahmad said. "Because women and children were slaughtered. Because some ran—and others sold the place piece by piece."

A door opened. A man stepped out, a girl clutching his cloak. He had a neat beard and his left wrist wrapped in cloth.

"Hunter," he said, smooth. "Come inside. Speak like men. Don't frighten the children."

"No," Ahmad said. "We speak here. All will hear."

Faces appeared at shutters and doorways. Ahmad pointed to the wrapped wrist. "Show it."

The man hesitated, then peeled it back. The skin was pitted, eaten by lime.

"You led them," Ahmad said.

The man forced a laugh. "I showed a spring. Water is mercy. Would you refuse mercy?"

Voices stirred.

"You marked stones," Ahmad said. "You cut trees. You took their bread."

A farmer shouted: "He came home with meat when we had none!"

Another: "He walked with them at night!"

A woman: "He told them which wall had no men!"

The man spat dry. "Lies. You only want someone to blame."

"Don't make me count," Ahmad said, voice sharp.

The man's excuses came faster. "The Franks would've found it anyway. They are many, we are few. I have children—would you starve them? Wouldn't you do the same?"

"No," Ahmad said.

The word cracked through the square. Nahhas padded forward, silent.

Ahmad reached for his quiver. He lifted one arrow high so all could see the iron tip.

"For every arrow I give the Franks," he said, "nine will be kept for the traitors."

He said it once. Then louder. The square repeated it: first a farmer, then another, then a chant building—"Nine for the traitors! One for the enemy!"

The man with the scar tried to drag the girl back inside. "Who are you to judge me?" he shouted. "Aleppo,

Damascus—did they come to help? Why not roar at their gates?"

Ahmad stepped closer, forcing him into the open. "Because you were here. Because your chalk was on our stones, your hands on our bread, your feet on our paths while our dead lay unburied. You were ours. That makes you worse."

Two men stood from the bench. They didn't look eager, but they grabbed him by the arms. He fought once, then sagged. They dragged him to the flat stone where meat was cut on good days. The girl sobbed, pulled back by a woman.

Ahmad stood over him. "If any here would say I am wrong, speak now."

Silence.

The man's lips moved in broken prayer. Then he tried rage. "You are nothing! A hunter with beasts! A savage! The lords will crush you!"

Ahmad hauled him to his knees. "You should have feared Allah."

He drove the arrow into his chest. Once. Twice. Again. The shaft cracked but he hammered it down, iron biting flesh. The square counted—five, six, seven. The old man croaked eight. At nine, silence.

The traitor slumped. His chest was black with blood, eyes glassed.

Ahmad wiped his hand on the dead man's cloak. He turned to the square. "This is the price of betrayal. Remember it. Feed them, guide them, excuse them—you'll pay it."

Faces were pale. Some nodded. Some turned away. Fathers made sons watch.

Ahmad faced them all. "Hide your jars in the old channels. Bake two breads—one to carry. Don't light fires on the ridge. Move at dawn. And if they ask the way, send them wrong—or send them to me."

Reeh dropped to his glove, beak clicking. Men flinched. Nahhas prowled back to his knee.

Ahmad crouched before the boy who had pointed earlier. "Do you have a sling?"

The boy nodded. Ahmad showed him how to seat the stone. "Stone to the knee. Then run. If you can't kill, make a man limp. Limping men do less harm."

The boy's face lit with pride.

Ahmad straightened. He looked once at the woman holding the girl, then turned away. "His sin is not yours."

No thanks came. None was needed.

Ahmad mounted Adham. Wolf and hawk fell in. As he rode out, a chant rose behind him:

From the ridge he glanced back. The villagers dragged the body to the earth. A stone would mark the spot. But it was the lesson that mattered. Words would travel farther than bones.

Let the people know.

He turned south. There were others on his list.

CHAPTER 7 — THE COWARD'S LESSON

The road bent south into country that should have sent men to Ma'arra but had not. Ahmad knew the name of the place before he saw it. Every refugee on the road spat it when asked who had failed them. An amir there had sworn in the mosque to send horsemen—and then kept them in his yard like tethered cattle.

Ahmad rode slow into the valley. Adham's hooves drummed on the hard track, Nahhas trotted ahead with his head low, and Reeh wheeled above. The people in the fields saw him coming. They stopped cutting barley, stopped their chores, and simply stood. A hunter with beasts at his side did not come into a valley unless he meant something.

The village sat close around a low fort—mud brick walls patched and thin, a gate with planks old enough to splinter at a knock. The fort looked proud enough to its own people but small to anyone who had stood on Ma'arra's stones. Smoke curled from cook pots. Chickens scratched the dust. Nothing about the place said war.

Men at the gate reached for spears, then froze when they saw who it was. They knew the wolf, they knew the hawk, and they knew the name that walked ahead of both.

"Father of Beasts," one whispered, too loud not to carry.

Ahmad swung down from Adham and let the reins fall. The stallion stood without tether. He walked forward and the guards stepped back, not from respect but because fear moved their feet before thought. Nahhas padded behind him, shoulders rolling like a waiting blow.

"I want the amir," Ahmad said.

The guards didn't answer, but one ran. The rest held their spears upright, knuckles white. Ahmad stood in the gate's shadow until the runner returned.

The amir appeared at the head of the court steps. He was a heavy man in a fine robe and a poor face, the kind that folds itself into excuses before the mouth even opens. A cluster of his men stood behind him, swords sheathed. Villagers filled the square, called by rumour faster than by voice.

Ahmad spoke so all could hear. "Ma'arra called. You swore. You promised horsemen. None came."

The man spread his hands. "Lion of the mountains—Ma'arra fell in days. Even had I sent men, what would a few dozen do against a host that eats towns in a week? Better to keep them here, to guard our own. Had I thrown them away, you would call me fool instead of coward."

"You are wrong," Ahmad said. "Better a fool who stood than a coward who sat."

His men shifted uneasily. The villagers said nothing.

Ahmad stepped forward. "Your excuses are meat for dogs. You hid behind your walls while others starved. You let our women burn so your bread would not be light."

The amir's mouth tightened. "I did what any ruler would. My duty is to my own people first."

"No," Ahmad said, voice carrying sharp. "Your duty is to Allah, to justice, to those who died while you ate. You sat in comfort while they boiled flesh in Ma'arra."

The man flushed. "You speak like a madman. I owe you no account."

"You owe the blood of Ma'arra an account," Ahmad answered.

He moved. Fast. His fist cracked across the man's jaw, sending him stumbling down two steps. The crowd gasped. Nahhas growled once, deep and low, but every sword stayed sheathed, the truth was apparent.

Ahmad followed, seized the collar, and dragged him into the square. "Stand."

The amir tried to bluster. "You will regret—"

The back of Ahmad's hand shut his mouth. Blood touched his lip.

"Take it," Ahmad said. He struck again, open-handed. "This is for Ma'arra."

The crowd stirred. Some flinched. Others leaned forward.

"Take it!" Ahmad's voice grew harder. He kneed the man in the belly and let him fold. "This is for the children burned."

The man gasped, tried to curl. Ahmad hauled him up by the beard.

"Take it!" He punched once, twice, until blood ran down over the fine robe. "This is for the men who died waiting for you."

The amir sagged. Ahmad let him fall in the dust. His men shifted, but froze as Nahhas stalked a pace forward, hackles high. Reeh stooped low once, a black cut across the sun, and all eyes followed her instead of their master.

Ahmad looked at the crowd. "This man swore in the mosque to send riders. He did not. He let oaths rot. He kept his sons safe while your relatives were killed. Is this an amir—or a hyena?"

The villagers murmured. A few spat.

Ahmad kicked him lightly to rouse him. "Stand."

The man groaned, smeared his own blood on the stones as he pushed himself up.

"Look at them," Ahmad shouted. "Look at your people."

The man raised his head, swollen-eyed.

"Their families died while you hid! Tell me—why?"

The words came out broken. "Because I feared."

"Louder!"

"Because I feared!"

The admission carried. Ahmad dropped him back in the dust.

"There. Your amir admits it. Fear of men ruled him. If fear is his master, let him sit with the women and children. Hire a wet nurse to suckle him, since he fears standing."

Laughter cracked the silence—bitter, but laughter all the same. Men who had lost brothers let it out. Women nodded tight-lipped.

Ahmad spat beside him. "That is your lesson. When the Muslims call, answer. When their blood is spilt, then rise. Or be disgraced in this life and the next."

He turned to the villagers. "Teach your sons to sling stones. Hide your bread. Do not trust oaths from men who fear the creation. Do not hide while others cry for help."

He whistled. Reeh swept to his glove. Nahhas returned to his heel with a growl still under his breath. Adham stamped once at the gate.

Ahmad mounted. He looked once more at the square. The man lay on his side, robe torn, too shamed to rise. His men had not moved to help him.

Ahmad's voice cut across them. "Remember: for Ma'arra, for the dead. Fear is a coward's excuse. You live only by what you stand for."

He turned Adham and rode out. Whispers followed him up the road. Some called him lion. All knew what they had seen: a man who did what their amir had not, who spoke what none else dared.

Behind him, the amir's name would taste of shame for years. And those who had excused their silence now felt it burning in their own throats.

CHAPTER 8 — BLOOD AND BETRAYAL

The road was rutted from weeks of wheels and hooves. Dry grass leaned flat, beaten into dust by too many feet. Ahmad kept to the rise above it, moving where rock and scrub gave cover. Adham climbed sure-footed, ears flicking at every sound. Nahhas loped ahead, low and silent. Reeh circled in a wide wheel overhead, black against the sun.

He had been told whispers in a small village. A handful of men were seen walking with the enemy — not pressed slaves, not captives, but walking shoulder to shoulder, showing the way through gullies and pointing toward springs. Men of our land guiding strangers. Some even smiled.

When Ahmad heard it, his blood had settled heavy and cold. This was worse than cowardice. This was feeding the foxes with your own sheep.

By mid morning, he saw them.

Down on the road, a small party moved slow. Four Franks in patched mail, spears upright, crossbows slung.

Two locals walked with them, cloaks pulled back, hands free, not bound. They had a cart with a sway-backed mule, the wheels squealing. The cart was stacked with sacks and amphorae — grain, maybe oil. Enough to feed a village for weeks.

Ahmad dropped to one knee behind a rock and watched.

The two locals laughed at something one of the Franks said. They pointed to the ridge, to the folds in the land, showing shortcuts. One reached out and clapped a Frank on the arm like a brother. The mule brayed, hushed with a stick.

Then Ahmad heard it.

One of the locals raised his hand and said in Arabic, loud, almost proud:

"God wills it."

The Franks barked back their own cry in their tongue: "Deus vult!"

The sound hit Ahmad like a stone in the chest. Different words, same meaning. He had never heard them together before. Now he knew. The invaders and the collaborators had joined voices.

His jaw clenched until it hurt. His hand closed around the fletching of an arrow.

Enough.

He stood, smooth and deliberate, drawing the bow in the same breath. The string snapped forward. The first arrow slammed into a Frank's throat before the man had time to lift his shield. A second arrow flew before the others even turned — it buried itself in the chest of another Frank, pitching him backward over the cart.

"Wolf!" Ahmad hissed.

Nahhas sprang from the scrub like a shadow with teeth. He tore into the legs of the third Frank, dragging him down before he could raise his crossbow. The man's scream was cut short when the wolf's jaws closed on his neck.

"Go!" Ahmad shouted, and Reeh stooped from the sky. Her talons raked across the eyes of the fourth Frank, who shrieked and dropped his spear, stumbling blind.

By the time Ahmad reached the road, sword out, the Franks were already broken. He finished the blinded man with one slash across the face, steel cutting through bone. Nahhas shook the last until silence, blood spattering the dust.

The two collaborators froze. One bolted toward the rocks.

Ahmad ran him down in five strides. He slammed the man against the cart so hard the wood shook.
"You said it," Ahmad growled. "You raised your hand with theirs. You said it."

The man stammered, "Mercy! They promised food! No harm if we showed the way—"

Ahmad rammed him harder into the boards. "You showed them the way to our graves."

"I have children—"

"You should have died in place of Ma'arra," Ahmad spat, and drove the sword into his belly. He fell face-first into the dust.

The second man stayed on his knees, hands raised. "I only wanted to live."

Ahmad strode forward. "So did the children of Ma'arra." He cut him down in a single, unwavering arc.

Silence claimed the road. Only the mule shifted, stamping nervously beside the cart.

Ahmad checked the load: grain, oil, figs. Enough to keep many from hunger. Nahhas padded back, muzzle dark. Reeh settled to a post on the cart, feathers bristling.

Ahmad would not waste what people needed. He led the cart off the road, slow so the mule would not founder.

By late afternoon he reached a cluster of broken houses in the hills. The people stared hollow-eyed as he pulled the cart into the square.

"Take it," he said. "Grain, oil, figs. Bake bread, feed your children."

Hands shook as they reached for the sacks. A mother wept openly as she tore one open and let the grain run through her fingers.

Ahmad raised his voice. "This food was taken by those who walked with the enemy. It belongs to you. But do not hoard it. Share it with your neighbours. Share it with the next village, and the next. What I cannot carry, you must carry to them. No house should go hungry while another feasts."

The villagers nodded, murmurs spreading. Some whispered his name. Others just stared at the wolf, the hawk, the man who had brought food where there should have been only death.

Ahmad mounted again. Adham shifted under him, eager for the road. Nahhas trotted to his stirrup; Reeh wheeled high.

He looked back once. "Keep each other alive. Remember this. Allah says: The believers are but brothers, so make settlement between your brothers. And fear Allah that you may receive mercy."

The cart stood in the square, grain spilling like treasure, while Ahmad rode on.

EPIGRAPHS

"They marched from Ma'arra through our lands, leaving ruin behind them. Villages were emptied, fields stripped bare, and no tree remained uncut for their fires."
— *Ibn al-Athīr, al-Kāmil fī al-Ta'rīkh*

"So great was our want that we boiled horses' flesh and even the skins of beasts. Many among us perished on that march."
— *Fulcher of Chartres, Historia Hierosolymitana*

CHAPTER 9 — YOU BRING US A GIFT

Winter still clung to the hollows. Dirty snow sat in the shade like old cloth. The rest was mud and smashed grass—weeks of wheels and boots had turned the tracks into trenches. Ahmad kept to the high ground where rock and scrub gave cover. Adham climbed without fuss. Nahhas moved ahead, head low, a shadow with ears. Reeh traced slow circles until she was only a fleck.

He read the ground as he went. A wide path of deep ruts and hoof holes—main column. A lighter offshoot veering toward a line of tamarisks—runners or messengers. Fresh mule sign, one shoe split, heel dragging. He knelt and pressed two fingers into a print. Soft at the edge. Not an hour old.

He tied Adham in a fold of rock and went on with Nahhas. The wolf stalked from bush to bush. Voices reached them first—men speaking in the harsh music of the invaders, then a thinner voice answering in the tongue of the land.

Ahmad slid behind a boulder and looked down into a shallow field camp. A dozen Franks sat around low fires, helmets off, steam blowing from their mouths. A priest with a cut-down cross hung at his neck moved between cook pots. At the edge, under a leaning pine, a local man waited with his hood up. He spoke with his hands, showing turns in a road, pinching fingers to mark a spring, tapping three times toward a ruined orchard. A Frank with a black bird painted on his shield listened, nodded, then pointed south with two fingers and drew a curve in the air to show a detour.

No coins changed hands. Bread did. The collaborator ate it like a dog that expects a kick. When he turned to go, the Frank gripped his shoulder, said something short, and pressed two fingers to his own eyes, then pointed to the north ridge. The meaning was clear enough: watch there.

Ahmad slid back and circled to meet the man on the way out. He found the place without thinking—the kind of crease in the ground where sound dies and men go missing.

The collaborator came alone, hood down now, checking behind him every twenty steps. Ahmad let him pass, rose, looped a cord over his mouth, and pulled him backward into the scrub. Nahhas was there already, a breath at the man's ear, teeth close enough to chill skin. The man stiffened, tried to shout into the cord, and made only a wet grunt.

"Quiet," Ahmad said.

He tied the wrists. He didn't hit him. He didn't need to. He set the man on his knees with his back to a stone, then crouched close so the man could see the wolf and the glove and the calm in his eyes.

"You walk with them," Ahmad said.

The man nodded so fast the cord twitched in his teeth.

"You've done it before."

Another desperate nod.

Ahmad loosened the cord a finger's width. "Speak."

Words tumbled out. "Don't kill me. I can help. I can help."

"You've helped them," Ahmad said, flat. "You'll help us now. Start with this: the road south. How many on the forager lines? Where do they draw water? Who watches at night?"

The man swallowed air. "They split by threes. Dawn and last light. They carry empty skins from the lower stream, under the two broken figs. Their sentries—north side is thin after midnight, by a burnt orchard with five stumps. They don't like the ground there. They say it eats feet."

"Signals?"

The man glanced at Nahhas and found honesty. "Horn calls—one short for carts, two long for men down, three long and one short for fire. Hands too—open palm for 'hold,' two fingers for 'move.' I can show them."

"Where next?"

"South and a little east after the next new moon. Timber first. They're short. They'll cut in the high grove above the cisterns."

Ahmad let the silence sit. The man kept talking to fill it.

"They use a dark path through the thorn this side of the hill—no one watches it. And the officer with the bird on his shield keeps his own guard lazy. He trusts the priest to watch the fires. He—"

Ahmad lifted a hand and the words stopped.

"Say their words," Ahmad said. "The ones they shout before they move, the ones they use for counting, for water, for bread."

The man repeated a handful of sounds, clumsy and proud—bread, water, tomorrow, devil. He pointed as he said each, mimicking the invaders' mouths. Ahmad repeated them under his breath once, marking the shapes like cuts on wood. Not to understand—not yet—but to hold them.

"You know routes, habits, and a few of their words," Ahmad said. "You're good at staying alive."

The man nodded too hard. "I can help you. I can tell you when they march, who leads which pack, where they keep the oxen—"

"You'll tell someone," Ahmad said. "Not me."

Fear flashed again. "Please—"

Ahmad took an arrow from his quiver and stood it upright by the man's ear. He drew, aimed at the earth to the left, and loosed. The point struck so close the spray of grit salted the man's cheek.

Nahhas leaned and closed his teeth gently on the man's trouser leg. Not skin, not blood—just enough to let him feel the skull behind the eyes.

"You lie once," Ahmad said, low. "I let him finish."

"I won't. I swear." The man shook. "By Allah. By—"

"Save that," Ahmad said. He tugged the cord back into the man's mouth and stood. "Walk."

He put the rope around the man's waist and tied it to Adham's saddle horn. They moved by broken stone and scrub, staying off the road, sliding across frost at the edge of the fields. Twice Ahmad froze and dropped to a knee while a forager pair crossed below them. Once Reeh stooped short to draw a sentry's eye away from the line they travelled.

They reached a shepherd's camp as the light thinned. Ahmad asked, said little, and learned that men from Arqa had been seen riding a ridge the day before, looking north with hard eyes. Scouts. He moved again, pushing the pace until the prisoner stumbled and went to his knees. Ahmad yanked him up by the rope and kept going.

On the second night, a glow showed on the next ridge—a small, careful fire where no Frankish camp sat. Ahmad whistled once for Reeh to take height, waited, then sent a stone into the dark below the glow. A hiss answered, then a short rasp no Frank would use: two small strokes of steel on stone, then silence.

He stepped into the circle of low light with the rope in his hand. Two riders stood up from the rocks as if pulled by strings. Lean men, cloaks dark, bows strung. One had a scar like a hook at the corner of his mouth.

They looked at the wolf first, then at the hawk, then at Ahmad.

They greeted with Peace be upon you.

"Hunter," the scar-cheeked one said. "You bring us a gift."

"From your neighbours," Ahmad said, and pushed the prisoner forward. "He's a path into their camp. He knows their habits, their signals, their weak turns. Alive, he's worth more than dead."

The second rider stepped close to the collaborator with open contempt. "What did you sell for bread?"

The man mumbled into the cord.

Ahmad didn't look at him. He looked at the two riders. "Who commands you?"

"Arqa," the man said. "The amir's riders. Name's Qays."

Ahmad nodded once. "Then take him to your amir. Say to him from me: keep this coward breathing. Squeeze him for routes, words, and timing. The invaders' tongue will be a weapon if someone sharpens it."

Qays watched Ahmad with the kind of attention men reserve for tools they've wanted for a long time. "The amir's name is Abdullah," he said, almost testing how it sounded in Ahmad's mouth. "He'll want to hear from you as well."

Ahmad's answer was simple. "When I have something that uses the ground better than talk, I'll bring it."

Qays's partner cut the cord and the collaborator flooded the air with promises. Qays shut him up with a fist on the shoulder—not hard, just enough. "You lie, you die," he said without heat. "You don't lie, you live a little longer."

The man nodded until it seemed his neck might break.

Qays tied him to a pack saddle and tossed a cloak over his head. "What did he give you?" he asked Ahmad.

"Thin watch after midnight by a burnt orchard with five stumps. Foragers at dawn and dusk. Water under two broken figs. Horn calls—one short carts, two long men down, three long and one short for fire. A quiet path through thorn. A lazy captain with a bird on his shield who trusts a priest to watch the flames. Timber next, then south-east on the new moon."

Qays's eyes shifted as he turned each piece in his head. "We'll use it."

"Use him too," Ahmad said. "Teach someone his words. Make a list. When I come to Arqa, I'll hear them."

Qays nodded once. "You'll be welcome at our fire."

Ahmad glanced at the tied man. "If he tries to run, hold him in the dark and let him listen to the wolf breathe. He'll learn faster."

For the first time, Qays laughed. "I'll remember that."

They doused the small fire with a palm of dirt. The night took shape around them again. Reeh shifted on her perch and settled. Nahhas stared at the collaborator until the man looked away and kept looking away.

Qays swung up into the saddle. "There's a place two ridges over where the ground eats hooves. If you want to hurt them without losing men, you'll find it."

"I know it," Ahmad said. "I watched a cart break there today."

"Then we're already reading the same page," Qays said. He touched a heel to his horse and moved off, his partner behind him, the collaborator tied between.

Wind moved over the ridge, dry and cold. Down in the dark, a horn sounded once in the invaders' camp—short and bored. Ahmad listened, then repeated the sound in his mind until he could have drawn it with a knife.

He set a hand on Adham's neck and felt the horse's steady warmth. He whistled once to the hawk and she lifted, then drifted back to his glove for a breath before taking height again.

There was work now that wanted a map in the head: a thin picket at a burnt orchard; water under two broken figs; a hidden path through thorn; horn calls with meaning; a road that would carry an army at the dark of the moon.

Ahmad turned his face toward the hills and moved. He didn't look back. He didn't need to. Behind him, a coward would reach Arqa alive. Ahead of him, the ground was already telling him where to cut.

CHAPTER 10 — BETWEEN MARKETS AND PRAYER

Morning light filtered through bare branches as Ahmad crouched in a pocket of scrub beside a stream. Nahhas pressed his great head into Ahmad's hands, rumbling with pleasure while the hunter scratched the wolf's ruff and rubbed behind one scarred ear.

"You kept me standing yesterday," Ahmad said, voice low. "You always do."

A soft thump landed on his head. Reeh. The hawk's claws sank into his hair like she owned it. She bent and tapped his forehead with her beak, starving for attention.

"All right, little queen," he said, tipping his head so she could nudge the crown of it. He ran two fingers along her head, then behind her neck where she liked it most. Reeh closed her eyes and made a pleased sound.

Adham protested from the stream, as if reminding them he existed. Ahmad stood, crossed to the stallion, and stroked the black neck, palm to muscle.

"You carried me through the ash," he murmured. "You'll carry me farther yet if Allah allows."

For a minute, there was nothing but this small family and the cold water. Then he shouldered the day. He checked the bowstring, tightened the hawk's jesses, and slung the empty feed-bag across the saddle. Time to trade.

The land south of Arqa ran softer than the high country—richer soil, lower ridges, villages tucked like nests into folds of earth. The main host had passed this way: cut beams, hacked hedges, wells with severed ropes. Ahmad stayed on lesser tracks that skirted orchards and old terraces, entering a hamlet from the open instead of bursting through a lane. Fear grows from surprise. He would not arrive as a raider.

Children saw him first and froze. The wolf at his stirrup, the hawk on his fist, the black horse—stories had outrun him. Women stepped to doorways and went still. Men by a low market ring of stones set down their tools and watched.

"I come to trade," Ahmad called plainly. "Nothing else."

That broke the air. A few stalls creaked open—reed mats, patched awnings, thin tables. A smith with burn-scorched beard. A leather worker. Two grain-sellers with little to sell.

Ahmad swung down and set trophies on the stones: two Frankish swords, nicked and dull; a bent helm; a small mail shirt crusted with smoke.

"I need a blade," he said to the smith, direct as a hammer. "Curved. Damascus work. No gilding. Balance forward enough to bite, light enough to draw twice. Good steel, no show."

The smith looked from the wolf to the hawk to the man and decided to treat him as a buyer, not a tale. He went to a chest and unwrapped a blade in old cloth—a Damascus saif (sword) with a tight pattern in the steel. No ornaments. Only a line of fuller that promised the cut.

Ahmad lifted it, swung once, reverse and return, then checked the weight with a short wrist cut. He eyed the edge. "This will do."

"Anything else," the smith said.

Ahmad tipped the Frankish pieces with a boot. "These, plus arrowheads and a file."

The smith's jaw moved, counting in his head. "Add the helm and I'll include a quiver. Stitched tight. No fray."

"Done."

They sealed it by hand, not word. Ahmad slid the new blade home into a plain scabbard. He tried the draw: clean. The re-sheath: smooth. He took a small bundle of bodkin points, a flat file, and a pot of oil for strings.

From the leather worker he chose a new bow-grip and a spare sling pouch. From a fletcher's basket—a surprise—he picked twenty good shafts, straight-grained, fletched tight. He paid with a Frankish dagger and a length of chain.

The grain-sellers brought a single sack forward and apologised with their eyes. Ahmad shook his head. "Keep it. You'll need it more than I will."

Whispers knitted around him, not fearful now, only intent. A boy edged closer than his mother liked, wide-eyed at Nahhas. "Does he bite?" the boy blurted.

"If he must," Ahmad said. "Not if you're wise."

The boy's hand hovered. Ahmad nodded once. The boy touched thick fur and sucked in a breath at the warmth beneath it. Reeh, jealous of attention, hopped from Ahmad's fist to his head again. This time a few men laughed, surprised at the sight of a hawk sitting like a spoiled cat on the "Father of Beasts."

"Show-off," Ahmad told her, with a smile. Reeh clicked as if agreeing.

By the stream he worked fast: oil on bowstring; file on a nick in a hook; check of Adham's hooves; burrs pulled from Nahhas' coat. Quiet, practical care. The kind that keeps a man and his beasts alive.

An elder with a staff approached, flanked by two others. "Word comes from the north," he said. "Arqa is ringed. Tents like fungus after rain. They've been there a few days. Some say a week."

"How many?" Ahmad asked.

"Too many." The elder glanced at Nahhas and lowered his voice. "Will you go there?"

"Yes."

"You'll find little safety and less food."

"I'm not going for food," Ahmad said.

The elder searched his face for a long moment and found whatever he needed to find. He inclined his head. "If any pass this way fleeing, we'll take them in. If any wear white cloth with red marks, we'll vanish into the hills."

"Good," Ahmad said simply.

He carried water to the bank and washed—hands, mouth, nose, face, beard, arms to the elbows, hair, ears, then feet—slow and exact. He spread his cloak on clean ground near a tree. Nahhas lay down and guarded behind him with his chin on his paws; Adham grazed; Reeh circled once and settled on a branch to watch.

After he finished, Ahmad raised his hands. He didn't speak long. "Allah, have mercy on the weak. Strengthen the hands that will defend the weak. Keep my aim true and my path straight."

After some time, a woman near the stream made space for him to pass. "They call you many things," she said. "Whatever you are, may Allah guide your path."

"If Allah Wills," he answered.

He strapped the new blade tight, slung the quiver, checked the hawk's jesses, and swung into the saddle. The stallion felt the change in him and arched his neck. The wolf rose, ready as ever. The hawk took to the air.

Ahmad looked once around the small market—at the boy who had dared touch a wolf, at the smith who had traded good steel, at the women who had not panicked when a man with beasts walked in. Then he turned Adham toward the south road.

"Arqa," he said to no one and to all of them.

He didn't think twice. He didn't ask for help. He set the stallion to an easy trot and let the village fall behind, a thin curl of smoke rising clean in the morning air. Ahead, somewhere beyond the low ridges, a ring of firelight and banners waited around a stubborn city. He would go and stand where he could make the most hurt with the least waste, and if men wanted a story to tell about the "Father of Beasts," they could tell it after the work was done.

CHAPTER 11 — VOICES IN THE CITY

The walls of Arqa stood pale against the night, their battlements bristling like the back of an old wolf that still had teeth. The enemy host ringed the city in tents and smoke, but Ahmad slipped between their watch fires, low in the saddle on Adham's back.

He moved like a hunter who knew patience was survival. Reeh circled high, a black fleck against the stars. Nahhas trotted at his stirrup, ears twitching at every sound. They had lived this game before—passing where men saw nothing, breathing where no one expected breath.

At the northern gate a guard opened without a word. The man lifted his torch just enough to glimpse the wolf's flank and the hawk on Ahmad's arm. He smiled and turned the flame aside. Some doors opened not with passwords, but with fear and faith together.

Inside, the air smelled of smoke and thin cooking. Days of siege had already made the city weary. Lamps burned low, hearths gave little heat. The streets pressed close, crooked and shadowed. Ahmad led Adham through them, hooves scuffing softly.

Children saw him first. They always did. A barefoot boy whispered a name: Father of Beasts. His sister clutched his sleeve, but she stared wide-eyed at the wolf padding beside Adham. Nahhas sat, watching the children without moving.

Ahmad swung down and crouched, lowering himself so the wolf looked less like death. "He bites only those I tell him to," he said, his voice rough but steady. "Do you want to touch his coat?"

The children looked to their mother. Her face was gaunt, carved by hunger, but she nodded. The boy reached out with a trembling hand and brushed Nahhas' ruff. The wolf did not stir. The girl touched next, and her laugh—thin and high—carried farther than it should have in those streets.

More faces appeared in doorways. Men muttered, women whispered prayers. One spat the word jinn into the dust, but no one blocked the way. Ahmad rose, cloak heavy on his shoulders, and led Adham on. The people made room without being asked.

At the square, he found familiar faces: fighters he had met on the road when he handed over the collaborator. Among them was Qays, scar still fresh along his cheek. He grinned when he saw Ahmad.

"Peace be upon you, and the mercy of Allah, and his blessings."

"You were right to spare him," Qays said. "The prisoner's been speaking. Our amir, Abdullah has him watched day and night. Already we've learned how their supply convoys move."

Ahmad smiled but he said nothing.

By the stables, stray cats prowled in the shadows, thin and desperate. Ahmad crouched and broke what little bread he had, scattering crumbs in the dust. The cats darted forward, mewling, and pressed against his hands as he stroked their backs. Adham stamped, jealous, until Ahmad rubbed his muzzle. "We must think of others," he murmured. Nahhas huffed, in acknowledgement. Reeh fluttered down, landing squarely on his head and pecking at his hair until Ahmad scratched the feathers at her neck. The men nearby chuckled, the sound carrying warm for the first time in days.

That night, word was sent to the amir, Abdullah that the Father of Beasts had entered the city.

When the call for prayer came, Ahmad prepared. But water was now forbidden for purification; every drop had to be saved. By Abdullah's order, the faithful used the dust of the ground instead. Ahmad pressed his palms to the floor and lifted them to his face and arms. It was enough. He spread his cloak on the stone and prostrated to his lord.

Nahhas sat steady at his back. Adham lowered himself onto his haunches beside him, snorting once as if to share the prayer. Reeh hopped down and began tugging gently at the stallion's mane until Ahmad reached up and stroked her feathers when he finished. The men watching could not help but laugh softly again.

Ahmad prayed aloud:

"O Allah, give perseverance to those inside these walls. Give fear to those who march with shaytan (satan). Do not let Ma'arra be repeated."

When he rose, grey light was climbing the walls. Beyond them, banners stirred in the morning wind, and the siege pressed closer.

EPIGRAPHS

"If the rulers of Syria had been united, the Franks could never have stood before us. But each thought only of his own walls, and so the land was torn open for them."
— *Ibn al-Qalānisi, Damascene chronicler (12th century)*

"They quarrelled more than they fought. Their swords were for each other's pride, not for our throats."
— Albert of Aachen, *Historia Hierosolymitanae expeditionis* (early 12th century)

CHAPTER 12 — THE PRISONER'S TONGUE

The first week of the siege had taught Arqa to sleep light. Horns sounded at odd hours. Drums thudded. Ladders tested stone, then scraped away. The city tightened its belt and watched.

Ahmad stood on the north wall with a bow in his hand and smoke in his throat. Reeh circled above him, small and dark against a pale morning. Nahhas lay behind the crenel, head on paws, eyes never still. Below, the enemy camp spread like a rash—ditches, mounds, raw wood, cook smoke, crosses on cloth.

A ladder came up too fast at a weak angle. Men in white tunics rushed it as if speed could replace sense. Ahmad loosed. One man folded at the rung; another dropped his shield; the ladder wobbled and went over backwards. Stones followed it. Someone cheered, then caught himself and saved his breath.

A horn blew to the west. The pressure shifted. The enemy tried there next. Typical: feel for soft wood, press until it creaks.

"Rotate," Ahmad said. "Two merlons down, take their place."

He crossed behind the line, counting—arrow bundles, jars, hands that shook and hands that did not. No one had extra of anything. No one complained.

A runner came up the stairs two at a time. "Father of—" He stopped himself, swallowed. "Ahmad. The amir sends for you."

Ahmad nodded. "Hold this line. Save arrows. Stones do work." He whistled. Reeh rose to a higher circle. Nahhas stood and stretched, then fell in at Ahmad's heel as he left the wall.

The streets below had that tight look towns get when they're not sure how long they'll last. Doors half-open. Fires banked low. Children quiet because the adults were. Ahmad passed a well with a line of jars and a guard who watched water like it was gold. It was.

At the keep's side tower a door stood open and two spear men stepped aside without being told. Word runs faster than feet. Inside, the air was cooler, the light thinner. A table had been dragged into a long room. Maps lay on it—scratched lines for ridges, pebbles for towers, a coil of rope marking the enemy ditch. Men stood around the table with the set faces of people who'd slept badly and were pretending they hadn't.

Abdullah was not a large man. He wore a plain coat, a sword that had seen labour, and the look of someone who listened before he spoke. He lifted his chin to Ahmad in greeting, then glanced down, not at the man, but at the wolf and the hawk-shadow that crossed the slit of a window.

"Ahmad," he said. "Thank you for coming."

"You sent for me," Ahmad said.

Abdullah nodded to a guard. "Bring him."

They brought the collaborator from the cell—wrists bound, ankles in a short hobble. He walked because he had learned it was better than being dragged. When he saw Ahmad, he flinched like a horse that remembers the bite of a rein. His eyes went straight to Nahhas, then to the bow in Ahmad's hand, then to the empty space at Ahmad's belt where a blade might live.

"Do not leave me with him," the man blurted to Abdullah's men. The plea made half the room look from the prisoner to Ahmad and measure them both again.

"No one is leaving you," Abdullah said. "But you will answer."

The prisoner answered before the question. "I will tell. I will tell all."

Ahmad said nothing. He set Rech's jesses on his fist. The hawk settled, bright-eyed and calm. Nahhas simply stood, silent, the kind of silence that shortens lies.

Abdullah gestured to the table. "Show us."

The prisoner leaned over the rough map. His bound hands made a clumsy shape. "They'll dig here." He tapped the rope coil. "Ditch, then mound. They mean to bring one high tower to the west gate where the ground rises." He pointed to a small pile of pebbles. "They'll gather wood in the olive stands... and they'll have a side camp of sick men here. They call it"—he fumbled for the sound—"'lazaret'."

"Guard numbers?" Abdullah asked.

"They change," the man said, words tumbling. "At night, a watch every fifty paces. In the small hours they thin. Dawn they beat the drums and swap men. Their word for dawn—" He looked at Ahmad and tried to shape it with his mouth. "Mat... tins. And they say 'north' with a hard 't'. Nor'th. The ones who speak for them—Greek, some—use different words. But I can tell you the rhythm. Water. Wood. Prayer. Dig. Eat. Dig. Always the same."

Ahmad watched the man's eyes. Fear made people talk. Real memory made them look right and left as if searching for a thing they had actually seen. He was searching.

"Officers?" Ahmad asked.

"They wear the better mail," the man said, relief at a question he could answer. "And red cloaks when they boast. One rides a grey horse with a clipped tail. He beats men with a staff when they lag. He trains them by the ditch in lines. He is often at the mound in late afternoon. He shouts at the carpenters. He likes to look taller than the boards."

"Supply?" Abdullah said.

"They haul grain from the north and cut beams from the west," the man said. "Small parties go for water at the stream by the fig terraces. They say 'water' with a round mouth. Woa-ter." He formed the sound clumsily.

"When they speak of the tower ropes, they use a word that sounds like 'rayn'. Rain. Rope."

Ahmad filed the sounds. He did not need a tutor. He needed anchors for ears on dark ground.

Abdullah pointed to the rope coil that marked the ditch. "Depth?"

"Deeper each day," the man said. "They lay planks and drag them forward so men don't sink. They are clumsy at night. Torches make them brave and blind."

A scrape sounded at the slit window. Reeh hopped off Ahmad's glove to the sill, then back, then to a beam above, as if the room belonged to her. Men smiled without meaning to. The prisoner swallowed.

Abdullah looked to Ahmad. "We have used him to glean times and habits. He says their foragers move on the second day after rainfall, when their mules find better footing. He says they falter at false alarms near dawn because their priests pull them back to sing. True?"

Ahmad nodded once. "I've seen the thinning."

"We plan to hurt their ditch and frighten their wood parties," Abdullah said. "Strike before the tower grows."

He slid a small pouch across the table. "Powdered lime. In the dark it blinds men who think water will wash it away."

"We have little oil," another captain said. "Pitch less. But we've saved some for the tower's rungs."

"Not for fire," Ahmad said. "For grip. Grease rungs they're climbing, not for burning. A man who falls on his own is a better lesson than a man who cooks."

Abdullah's mouth twitched—approval without smile. "What else?"

Ahmad pointed to the fig terraces north of the enemy's water parties. "Archers on the lip. Let goats loose behind them at my signal to stir dust and look like numbers. Ambush the return, not the fetch. Mules panic more on the way back because the men relax when they think the danger has passed."

A captain with scarred knuckles grunted. "I like that."

Ahmad tapped the map again. "At night, peg-ripping. Cut one in four, not all. Leave tents that sag. A sagging tent makes a man curse his own ropes. He doesn't see the man behind him."

Abdullah turned to the prisoner. "When do they change watch on the west ridge?"

The man licked dry lips. He looked at Ahmad again, as if expecting teeth. "At first light, before they sing," he said quickly. "They grumble. They are slow."

"Good," Abdullah said. He looked around the room. "Tonight we test them. Small. Clean. No dead left where they can see them at dawn—hide the work so fear grows. If we get prisoners, keep them alive for exchange."

He faced Ahmad. "You brought us one. He's been useful. We keep him breathing."

The collaborator nodded too fast. "Useful," he echoed.

Ahmad stepped closer—not looming, simply present. The man flinched all the same.

"You will talk again," Ahmad said quietly. "Not because you fear me. Because your friends will hang you if you go back to them with us in your mouth. Here you have a chance to pay for what you did and live."

The man gulped. "Yes."

Reeh shifted and made a soft chirp. Nahhas looked up without moving the rest of his body. The room had gone very still.

A guard knocked on the door frame. "Word from the north wall. Ladders again. They test, then pull back. Same two companies."

Abdullah nodded. "Hold rotation. No heroics. Save arrows, spend stones." He looked to Ahmad. "One more thing—language. Each time you hear a word from him, take it to the boys who watch. If they start to understand shouts, they'll move half a breath sooner."

Ahmad gave one short nod. He lifted his fist. Reeh dropped to the glove as if she'd been waiting for the cue.

As the guard led the prisoner back, the man blurted at Abdullah's shoulder, not daring to face Ahmad: "There is one more... their carpenters hide wedges under the tower wheels to stop it rolling back at night. If someone pulls them at the right moment—"

"—the tower sits in its own ditch," Ahmad finished.

Abdullah's eyes sharpened. "Good."

They broke from the room in twos, no crowding, no show. On the stair, two young fighters waited—Qays and Farid, sweat still drying at their hairlines, grins they hadn't earned yet and wanted to.

"Amir" Qays said, nodding. "We'll take the fig terrace."

"Take your slingers, not just bows," Ahmad said. "Stone to the knee. Limping men do less harm."

Farid's grin flashed. "I wish I was a father of beasts," he said, glancing at Nahhas and then up at Reeh.

"Your beasts would eat us by accident," Qays muttered.

"Allah gives us all what we can handle," Ahmad said, with a smile, and stepped past them.

Back on the wall, the air tasted of ash and sour water. Ahmad handed his bow to a boy whose fingers shook and watched the boy's hands stop shaking because a known weight had settled into them.

"Remember," Ahmad told the line, "Push ladders off with poles, don't lean your body over. They like to hook belts."

Nahhas sat at his back, not circling, just there. Reeh took her high circle again, a moving point every eye below would catch without knowing why.

Across the ditch, drums thumped. A priest's voice rose and fell. The enemy moved boards, rolled a wheel, then stopped to argue about a wedge. Ahmad couldn't hear the words, not yet, but he had the rhythm. He had a map in his head that would be sharper by nightfall.

Behind him, the city breathed in and out. Not famine. Not yet. Just rationed bread, careful water, quiet stoves. Fear had a place at every table, but it didn't eat everything. Not today.

A ladder scraped stone. Hands reached up. Ahmad nodded at the nearest men. "Push."

They pushed. The ladder went back. A man below cursed in a tongue Ahmad was beginning to recognise by sound if not by sense. He logged the shape of it, the bite of it, stored it with the others.

Tonight, they would test the ditch. After that, the wood parties. And after that, whatever the next day allowed.

He glanced once toward the keep. Abdullah would be at the table again, measuring risks, weighing small pains that bent big plans. The collaborator would be in a cell, not sleeping, hearing every distant bark of a wolf as if it were footsteps in the hall.

Ahmad set his feet, checked the line left and right, and looked outward. The enemy moved. So would he.

CHAPTER 13 — THE NIGHT HUNTER

The camp spread across the plain like a market that had forgotten daylight. Low fires burned to coals. Ropes ran from pegs to tent rings. Carts stood with their wheels chalked so they wouldn't roll. Helms hung at tent mouths, spears leaned together like bundled reeds. A few sentries walked their lines. The rest slept.

Ahmad watched from the ditch that fed the enemy's horse troughs. He wore a plain black cloak turned inside out to kill the shine. He'd rubbed soot into his hands and face and smeared animal fat along the cloak's hem so it would pick up dust and smell like the night. He meant to look like a beast, a shadow in the night that would trick men's eyes.

Nahhas lay flat in the reeds. Reeh rode the dark above them, a moving absence against the stars.

Ahmad listened first. Camp talk at night told you everything if you let it. A guard coughed. Somewhere a man muttered in his sleep. Leather creaked. A mule stamped. From farther off came a word he knew now:

"garde." Watch. Another voice answered, bored and close to sleeping on his feet.

"One man may not stop an army," Ahmad told himself, barely a breath. "But if they wake to shadows, I can weaken their resolve to fight."

He slid along the ditch to the first water cart. A barrel sat braced across it. A skin of congealed fat clung to the rim from whatever stew they'd made. He eased the lid, sniffed, and closed it again. If he spoiled the only drink at a post, men would talk to drown their fear. Better than arrows tonight.

He moved toward a triangle of tents where the ground dipped and sound died. A sentry stood there with a staff and a bell hung on a thong. The man's head nodded, woke, nodded again. Ahmad eased a sling from his belt, dropped a smooth stone in the pocket, and let it turn once. The stone flew. It struck the bell lightly enough to make a small chime. The sentry jolted, looked at it, and swore softly. Ahmad waited until the man turned away, then threw again—another faint chime, this time from the other side of the post. The sentry turned in circles, tapping the bell, grumbling. Good. Confusion without an enemy was better than a clean kill.

He left the trench and crawled into the tents, low and slow. Knots, ropes, pegs—this was a city of string. He cut two guy ropes near their pegs, left a third half-cut, and shifted one peg three hand spans. A light wind would do the rest. At the next tent he loosened the ridge-line one twist. No blaze, no noise—just sleep that would not hold.

A butcher's block stood by a cook fire gone to black. On the board lay a bowl of dark, half-jelled blood they hadn't thrown yet. He dipped two fingers, drew a wet hand print across the inside of a tent flap, and dragged a line knuckle-deep across a sleeping man's shield. He wiped the rest along the rim of a water jar and tilted it so the first pour at dawn would run red. If they blamed a devil, so much the better. If they blamed each other, better still.

A lone guard rounded a cart, shoulders hunched against the cold. Ahmad lay still until the man's boots were at his knee, then surged up, clamped a hand over his mouth, and pulled him behind a stack of hides. The knife slid under the jawline clean and fast. The body shivered and went slack.

Ahmad held him a moment longer, breathing steady, then went to work. He pushed the corpse under the hides, rolled a half-empty barrel in front of it, and smeared blood on the ground where the man had stood. He took the man's cloak, ripped the cross from it, and tied the torn cloth to a low branch behind the cart so it would brush faces at chest height. He dragged two lines of boot marks away from the scene and let them vanish into trampled earth. No body. Blood where a body should be. A story without an ending.

He circled to the picket line where the mules were tied belly-to-belly. He didn't cut the ropes; he loosened knots and twitched the lead just enough that a nudge would drop them. Then he took a leather strap, soaked it in the horse-trough, and snapped it three times—quiet, close. The nearest mule jolted and tangled. Hobbles slid. A stake popped. He walked away before the first curse rose.

Reeh drifted down to the lip of a cooking pit. Ahmad lifted a finger. She hopped to it. He fed her a sliver of meat and flicked his other hand toward a run of tent mouths. She rose without sound and skimmed the canvas, brushing a half-dozen guy-lines with her wings. Two pegs popped. One tent sagged at the corner. A sleepy hand reached out to fix it and found slack rope instead. A man swore, another shushed him, then swore back. Perfect.

At the grain carts he eased a chock and leaned a sack against a wheel so the whole breakfast pile would shift when the first man climbed it. He spilled a handful of grain into a footprint and scuffed it across the path toward the latrine trench. Let them wake to a mess and an argument about who slept on watch.

He saved the worst for last.

Near the centre of the camp stood a larger tent with a prayer board staked outside and a lantern shielded low. An officer's place—richer cloth, heavier ropes, better sleep. Ahmad snuck into the tent and found a sleeping officer, he helped him enter a permanent sleep and dragged his body away without a trace, only leaving some blood in his tent and no answers for his men. At the water cart beside it he lifted the lid and he poured blood inside. The first men to drink would believe it a punishment for them eating the bodies of dead Muslims or devil's sign.

On his way out he knelt by a small fire not yet dead and pressed a cross-marked scrap of cloth across the embers until it smoked. He lifted it, fanned it, then stamped the glow away and tucked the cloth under a pile of bedding. Not to burn men. To wake them coughing at nothing and make them drag everything into the night.

A patrol's footfalls came steady along the road—two men, one taller by the length of a head. Ahmad slid into the drain again, covered himself with a wet cloak, and let them pass. The taller one said a word he knew—"eau"—and tapped the barrel with his staff. "Water." The other laughed and said something about "diable." Devil. Ahmad felt his mouth harden. They would teach him the rest without meaning to.

When the patrol turned the corner, Ahmad raised two fingers and clicked softly with his tongue. Nahhas rose out of the reeds and padded into the gap between the outer tents and the carts. Ahmad pitched a pebble at a shield. Metal sang. A sleepy soldier sat up and peered. He saw nothing but canvas, rope, and dark. Then the wolf began to howl.

It wasn't a long howl. It was a sharp, close, downward roll that sounded too near for comfort and too far to strike. One, then silence. Another, from a different angle. Then a third that seemed to come from inside the carts. A man shouted. Another cursed him to be quiet. A tent corner gave way and sagged across three sleeping men.

One kicked free, stumbled into the next line, and dragged a peg with him. Rope hissed. Canvas dropped. Someone screamed as the tent pinned him. The mules began to pull and tangle. Stakes went, one after another. A lantern fell and flashed, then died under three boots at once. Now there were voices everywhere—questions with no answers.

Ahmad moved with the noise, always two tents away from the worst of it. He used the confusion to cross open ground and left some mayhem behind: a spear leaned to fall when touched; a shield moved so its owner would reach past the right one in panic; a stack of bowls shifted so the top plate would crash when the wind stirred.

"Enough," he told himself when the first horn blew short and angry. He had stayed long enough to be greedy. Greed killed hunters.

He slipped back to the drain, slid into the water, and let the chill bite him awake. Reeh dropped to his wrist without a sound. He felt her weight and steadied his breath. Nahhas met them at the ditch bend, licking one paw clean. Ahmad checked the wolf's pads with a touch and nodded. No cuts.

Behind them the camp's dark changed colour. Shadows moved against glow. Orders snapped. A man cried out when a water cup stained his face red. The cry became a scream that had nothing to do with wounds and everything to do with the mind.

Ahmad went out the way he came, then looped wide. He stopped once at a low rise and looked back. The camp wasn't burning. It was worse: it was awake, afraid, and busy. Busy men made mistakes before dawn.

He signalled Nahhas to howl long and loud into the dark so all who may have stayed sleeping would wake in a panic.

He reached the culvert below Arqa's wall while the stars still had their strength. Inside, the tunnel smelled of clay and old water. He took a breath, ducked, and climbed by handholds he already knew. At the top a guard hauled him the last half-arm and pressed him against the stone, hard and grateful.

"It worked," the guard whispered, eyes bright. "Their shouts are filling the silent night."

Ahmad only nodded. "Wake the captains at first light. Move the men where they can be seen from the camp. Make them look rested."

The guard grinned. "They'll think we slept."

"We did," Ahmad said. "They didn't."

He crossed the inner yard with a gait that hid the shake in his legs. The stable boy rose from a stool and reached for Adham's bridle before remembering himself. Ahmad rubbed the stallion's face, checked his hooves by feel, and let his forehead rest against the horse's for a moment. Then he knelt by Nahhas and ran a hand along his ribs. The wolf huffed, content.

He climbed the stair to a narrow room with a mat, a jug, and a garm he prepared earlier. Reeh hopped to the window beam and settled, head turning once, twice, then still. Ahmad changed his clothes and lay down without a care in the world.

He was asleep before the jug stopped rocking.

CHAPTER 14 — THE HUNTER AND THE HYPOCRITE

They let him sleep until the sun was high. A guard rapped softly on the lintel and slipped inside. "By Allah, they haven't slept the whole night," he grinned. "May Allah reward you for what you did."

Ahmad eased upright, joints answering the floor like old hinges. Nahhas lifted his head from the threshold, eyes bright; Reeh shuffled on the peg, then settled again.

Word ran ahead of them through Arqa's lanes. A baker's boy called, "Did you enjoy your sleep?" and two men at a well laughed: "Because the enemy did not!" Women smiled despite hunger; boys mimed a hawk stooping from a wall and a wolf's low lope beside a black horse. Ahmad nodded once to each and kept walking. He didn't hide the tired in his eyes, and he didn't apologise for it.

At the citadel, the guards on the door were already grinning. "Welcome, hunter. Did you rest well? Verily the enemy has moved slower and made many mistakes that cost them men while you slept."

Inside, the council chamber was warm with bodies and thin with food. Abdullah stood from his seat as Ahmad entered, no stiffness in it, only welcome.

"Peace, Ahmad," Abdullah said, taking his forearm. "You gave our walls a quiet night and gave the enemy none. May Allah make your strength a mercy for us and a thorn for them."

Laughter and low assent moved around the room. A captain called, "Did Allah grant you good dreams?" and another said, smiling: "He earned it."

Ahmad inclined his head. "If you wish, I can go out again tonight. There's more fear to be found."

A ripple of approval ran through the captains. "Can you do that?" Abdullah asked, teasing without doubt.

"Yes, and send a few men with me so I can train them to do the like of what I did, we can send them each night to different camps and leave them with no rest" Ahmad said, simple as a knife laid on a table.

"Then we shall," Abdullah said, amusement in his eyes. "May Allah make it easy for you to terrify them."

Not everyone laughed.

From the back, a thin voice cut across the warmth. The scholar—clean robe, careful beard, the same man whose words had already raised questions—stepped forward with the confidence of a man who mistakes cleverness for courage.

"So we trade in jinn now?," he said, pitching his voice to reach the rafters. "We let beasts walk our streets and praise tricks in the dark as piety. Is this the banner of

Arqa? Shadows and wolves? We should be speaking with the Franks, not goading them. They sent understandings—mercy for prudence, a gate for peace—"

He stopped too quickly, as if he had heard his own tongue slip. He tried to soften it, but the room had already gone still.

Abdullah's gaze hardened. "What 'understandings,' scholar?"

"Whispers carried on the wind," the man said, palms out. "What all cities speak of in siege. If we return to reason, they will meet at the west—" He swallowed. "—they will meet on fair terms. We need not bleed for pride."

Ahmad watched him a moment, the way he watched brush when a snake lay inside it. Then he spoke, voice even.

"Your words carry the weight of a swinging gate," he said. "I don't believe you speak for the good of your people, but only yourself."

The scholar forced a smile for the room. "I speak to save lives. You"—he flicked a contemptuous glance at Nahhas on the threshold—"parade carrion beasts and call nightmare a strategy. Children repeat your demon tales in the lanes. What will you do when the enemy answers in kind? When they burn us for your mischief?"

Ahmad walked three paces and was upon him before the man's breath changed. He did not draw steel. His open hand struck once, twice—sharp, controlled blows that took pride instead of teeth. The scholar reeled, caught himself on a pillar, blood bright at the corner of his mouth.

No guard moved. No captain flinched. A few faces looked disappointed only that they hadn't done it first.

"Listen," Ahmad said, low enough to make the room lean in. "At Ma'arra I heard promises like yours. I saw the pots after. You speak of deals like a man selling piss and calling it rain."

The scholar tried for arrogance and found only anger. "You threaten me in the amir's hall? You bring dirty beasts into places of purity? You invite their wrath—"

Ahmad's voice turned to iron. "I invite fear to the shaytan's camp as Allah commanded."

He took the scholar by the collar and pulled him close enough that only the front benches heard the next words. "When you talk, I hear Iblis (The Devil) himself. When you breathe, I smell the foul stench of a hypocrite." He let go, and the man stumbled back two steps.

Abdullah raised his hand—not to stop Ahmad, but to claim the moment.

"Enough," the amir said calmly, eyes on the scholar. "Your tongue has run ahead of your sense. You will answer for it."

He looked to the guards. "Take him. Bring any letters he wrote, and the names of those who carried them. Keep him alive. Allah's law will decide his punishment when this matter is clear."

The guards did not hesitate. They seized the scholar by the arms. He sputtered something about discreetness;

a captain in the doorway chuckled, "We'll see how discreet your pen was."

As they dragged him past, the scholar stared at Ahmad with a hatred that had no courage in it. Ahmad didn't give him a second glance.

Abdullah let the murmur swell and settle. Then he faced Ahmad again, all the warmth returned.

"Your work outside the walls breaks more spears than our stones," he said. "Tonight, go again. Keep them guessing which shadow holds teeth. We'll shift the watches to match—quiet feet on the parapets, no calls, no horns unless the fire catches. If you need men, take men, take only those that are confident with you. If you need none, go alone. And send word at dawn of what they fear next."

"I'll need the city to sleep early," Ahmad said. "No singing on the ramparts. No fires high. If they wake and see only darkness, their mind finishes the work."

"It will be done," Abdullah said. He added, almost laughing: "And when you return, we'll try to let you sleep more than the enemy."

A captain near the map table raised a hand. "Hunter—those words you said you're learning—their watch calls, the ones that mean shift and water. Do you know them now?"

"Enough to move when they think I don't understand," Ahmad answered. "The collaborator taught me more yesterday. Keep him alive—he's worth a dozen scouts."

"He lives," Abdullah said. "And he talks. Your name opened his teeth faster than any strap."

Laughter again—hard, satisfied. The room felt lighter than the food allowed.

As the council broke, men came to Ahmad in twos and threes, not to give advice but to take it. He spoke quickly, efficiently.

On his way out, a guard clapped his shoulder. "May Allah make it easy for you to terrify them."

Another, younger, grinned wide. "And if you can spare a nightmare or two, send one to the west trench."

Outside, the air was thin and bright. Nahhas fell in at his heel, satisfied by the scent of a man who'd been chosen, not questioned. Reeh hopped once to his glove, pinched the leather with her beak as if in approval, then lifted to the sky.

At the door, Abdullah called after him—half an order, half a joke: "Eat something before you go, Ahmad. We would keep you longer than the night keeps your enemies."

Ahmad nodded once. "Then I'll give the night back to us."

He stepped into the sun, the city around him already telling and retelling the morning: that the hunter slept while the enemy stared at darkness; that the amir laughed and said do it again; that a scholar's tongue had finally weighed enough to tip the law. Tonight would be more work.

And the walls, for the first time in days, felt taller.

CHAPTER 15 — THE LONG GRIND

Late winter bled into spring and the siege settled like a weight on every chest. By day, Arqa's walls held hard lines of men and boys. By night, the same men slept in their cloaks with hands for pillows and dreams filled with rest and glad tidings for the patient. Outside, the Frankish camp crept closer by ditches and brush screens; inside, rations tightened, tempers shortened, and watches doubled.

Ahmad moved between the two worlds. On the rampart he loosed clean and far, showing young bowmen how to draw to the ear and breathe through the shot. In the alleys he walked quietly, watching where fear gathered and cutting it away with short words and simple tasks. At dusk he traced the wall, marking the places where the enemy stacked hurdles too near dry thorns and where their sentries stood lazy in the lee of wagons. After dark he slipped out through a culvert with Reeh wheeling and Nahhas low to the ground, and he made sleep expensive.

He never did the same thing twice.

One night he unhooked hobble-ropes and slapped mules into the maze of tents; another he untied a run of guy-lines so a row of shelters sagged at once like teeth knocked from a jaw. He dragged a cart half a body-length and left wheel ruts pointing the wrong way. He moved boundary stakes so sentries answered the wrong shadows. He rolled closed barrels to new places and left open ones where rain would spoil them. Nothing loud; nothing brave; everything menacing.

He spread a new rumour the third week without saying a word. He took a dead man from the far picket line and buried him shallow under a trampled path, then let the heel of a boot show bone. By morning, men in that part of the camp walked in the ditch rather than on the earth. Two nights later he hung a cross-cloak high in a tamarisk so it clacked like bones when the wind turned. The sound travelled farther than any arrow.

The Franks' words began to make sense. He heard them at the gate and on the wind — aqua near the water-carts, porta in the mouths of officers, vigilia at the change of watch. He said them under his breath until they felt like tools. He used them once, softly, from a hedge — vigilia! — and listened while a tired sentry left his post and another took it, eyes averted. He moved past the empty place a minute later.

Inside the city, time left marks you could touch. The grain bins dropped to their chalk lines and then below them. Meals shrank to hot water with taste. Babies fussed less because they learned early that fussing won nothing. Women queued at the well with jars and stood in silence; nobody asked how much reached the bottom because every hand already knew.

There were names now to the men who had stood faceless along the parapet when Ahmad first climbed Arqa's wall. Qays, narrow and quick, ran messages along the walkways and never lost his breath. Sami, broad across the chest, kept lads laughing at the worst hours and slipped them stones when arrows ran thin. Nabil, a quiet archer with a careful eye, fletched through the night and never took credit for the straightest flights. And Farid—Farid with the easy grin—had a way of turning fear into a joke and jokes into courage.

After a hard press at the east tower, when the men came down shaking and short on words, Farid crouched five paces from Nahhas and lifted a hand like a man greeting an old friend.

"Careful," someone muttered.

Farid looked to Ahmad. Ahmad gave him the smallest nod.

Nahhas stood, weighing him, hackles half-raised. Farid didn't flinch. He held his hand there and let the wolf make the choice. After a long breath, Nahhas stepped forward, sniffed, then pushed his head under Farid's palm with a low huff that sounded almost like a sigh.

The courtyard let out a breath of its own. Farid scratched the ruff, grinning. "See? He knows a good man."

Qays snorted. "Your beasts would kill us by accident."

"They'd only try it once," Farid shot back.

Men laughed — a quick, bright sound that cut the cough of smoke in the throat. Ahmad said nothing, but one corner of his mouth moved. Nahhas finished with Farid and returned to Ahmad's side as if to remind everyone whose shadow he truly chose.

It wasn't all jokes. Abdullah, sent for Ahmad every few days with quiet questions and quicker thanks. They spoke standing over rough maps on a board held down with stones. Ahmad marked where the enemy's wagons bogged in wet ground and where their cooks set fires too near dry grass. Abdullah never wasted words. He listened, decided, and moved men without fuss.

In the second month, a runner brought Abdullah a folded scrap of parchment sealed with soft wax and a crude cross. To the wise within, it said in rough Arabic, open one gate and be spared. Water for peace. Bread for cooperation. It was like being offered a glass of poison sold as pure water.

Abdullah didn't show it to the council first. He sent Qays to fetch Ahmad.

"Your eyes," Abdullah said simply.

Ahmad read the shapes, then the air. "This is the second such letter," he said. "The first was burned on the wall by the market. The two hands are not the same."

Abdullah's jaw tightened. "We will find both."

They found one of them — the hypocrite scholar whose voice had curdled the mosque steps weeks earlier. He'd used a boy to carry a folded strip of calfskin to the ditch and drop it under a marked cedar stake. The boy never knew what he carried. The men who watched did.

The scholar went to a cell with a bucket and a blanket and a guard who didn't feel like speaking. He learned then what silence felt like when it belonged to others. He did not meet Ahmad's eyes when they passed in the corridor a day later. He stared at the floor and muttered verses at the stone. The guard said nothing. It was not yet his day.

Word reached from the prisoner Ahmad had captured and handed over weeks before — the collaborator. Kept alive, and worked by men who asked questions well, he had given routes, names of captains, and the hour they liked to change watch on the south ditch. He had also tried to tell stories to save his own skin; the scribes wrote the facts and let the stories fall to the floor. Ahmad took from him only what he needed: a handful of new words and the rhythm of the enemy's night.

The enemy's night grew worse.

One run of days, rain turned the camp to paste. Ahmad made it worse by tugging a pin here, nudging a brace there. A walkway folded in the small hours with a noise like a groan; men went into the slurry up to their waists and came up cursing. Another night, clear and cold, he left three small marks by three different watch fires, each with a single cross set wrong. He watched from a hedge while a priest mumbled prayers and fixed them, then walked a wide circle to check the other two and found them moved again, as if they had moved when his back was turned.

He never stayed to listen long; he didn't need to. The fear had weight. You could hear it in the way men carried spears and see it in the way they stared at the black between tents.

Inside the city, the long days wore grooves. Men learned to eat without looking at one another's bowls. Women learned new ways to stretch grain. Children learned to be quiet near the wells. The city didn't cry; it endured. And Ahmad brought back what he could from the enemy's camp, so did others.

Reeh found her own work. On still afternoons she took a high circle over the enemy camp and then stooped to a point on the far slope. She wasn't hunting meat. She was teaching men to look up and think about what looked back. Twice her shadow crossed a priest at prayer and his voice slipped on the note he held; twice it skated along the line of a patrol and one man walked into another because he watched the sky instead of the ground.

At the end of the second month, Abdullah stood with Ahmad on the western walk and watched the smoke drift south in a thicker line than before.

"Plague?" Abdullah asked.

"Sickness," Ahmad said. "And too many men sharing bowls."

He didn't smile when he said it. He didn't enjoy any of it. He only took note and filed each note where it would be useful.

The third month was heat and dust and short tempers. The enemy pulled their lines in, then out, then in again. Some days their horns sounded angry and close; other nights the songs died early and the fires burned small. Ahmad took the quiet as an invitation to wake them with Nahhas.

On a morning when the sun came up hard and white, Reeh landed on Ahmad's shoulder while he spoke with a knot of captains and shook herself like a wet dog, scattering small feathers. Farid laughed out loud. "If she lands on my head, does that make me Father of Beasts' uncle?"

"It makes you bait," Qays said.

"Bait gets fed first," Farid said, and men who hadn't slept a full night in a week still found the breath to grin.

That afternoon a cart of broken arrows turned into straight ones in the hands of Nabil and the boys he'd taught. Sami made a game of carrying water up the stairs on his shoulders without spilling a drop and shamed three younger men into trying it and doing it better than they thought they could. Small victories know their own way across a wall.

In the evenings on the wall, Ahmad found himself no longer alone. A small band of fighters gathered around Qays, the scarred captain who carried his weight like a wall of stone.

Farid was the loudest of them, always quick with a grin even in hunger. He tried once to coax Nahhas closer with a scrap of dried meat. The wolf bared his teeth, but Farid only laughed and said, "One day he will eat from my hand, and then you'll see I'm the true Father of Beasts." The men chuckled until even Ahmad's mouth tightened at the corner.

Yusuf, youngest among them, prayed every time before he strung his bow. His voice was sharp, his temper sharper, but when the arrows flew he steadied like a man twice his years.

Bilal spoke little, preferring to mend arrows in silence. But his bowstring was always tight, his shafts always straight. "A crooked arrow is worse than a coward," he said once, and no one argued.

Masud, oldest, carried a cough in his chest but his hands never shook. "If Allah keeps my grip, I'll not stop," he rasped. He treated the younger men like nephews, cuffing their heads one moment and shielding them the next.

Together they shared stale bread and the kind of laughter that carried farther than grief. Ahmad said little, but he listened. And when the night was thick and the torches burned low, he thought: these will be men to stand with when the road turns hard.

Near the end of that month, a runner from Abdullah's men found Ahmad where he was mending a bowstring. "The amir wants you," the man said, breathless.

In the small chamber, Abdullah stood over another scrap of parchment. The seal was broken. The words were the same as the first, only more desperate: Open one gate. Water for peace. Bread for... The script was the same hand that had touched the calfskin under the cedar stake.

Abdullah's eyes were dark and calm. "Jumua (Friday)," he said. "The judge will hear the proofs then."

Ahmad nodded once. He thought of the council chamber, of the scholar's tongue, of Ma'arra's ground. He had no speech to make about it. He only said, "I'll be there if Allah allows."

He left the chamber and crossed the courtyard. Nahhas rose from the shade and fell in at his knee. Reeh took the sky with a hard beat and climbed, a small mark against the late light. In the corner by the bake-oven, Farid scratched Nahhas once more, careful and quick, then stepped back when the wolf's gold eyes flicked his way.

On the wall, the enemy's songs started late and ended early. The wind came from the south and carried a sour note into the city. Men on both sides lifted water skins and drank slowly, not because anyone told them to, but because the body learns its lessons.

When the call to prayer came that evening, Ahmad washed with dust and prostrated with the rest. He asked for strength, to be showered in patience that would last longer than hunger and for fear to be sent to the enemy, not on to the brothers beside him. He rose, tightened his belt, and walked the line.

Friday was set. The people knew without being told. You could feel it in the way the market muttered and in how the guards at the gate watched the street instead of the field. The hypocrite sat on a straw mat and stared at the wall of his cell and moved his lips. No one answered him. Not yet.

Outside, a wheel snapped in the dark and men cursed in a language Ahmad now understood enough to map. Inside, Farid cleaned a cut on his knuckle with vinegar, hissed and then laughed at the pain. Qays folded and re-folded a strip of cloth until it lay like a straight road. Sami stacked stones to hold down a map that didn't need holding. Nabil ran his thumb along an arrow's shaft and smiled at how true it felt.

The siege did not end. It thickened. It pressed. It waited.

And Arqa waited back.

CHAPTER 16 — JUDGEMENT AT ARQA

Friday brought the city together. The mosque groaned with bodies pressed shoulder to shoulder, faces hollow with hunger but lit with the strength of prayer. The khatib's (speaker's) voice cut through the rafters:

"Be steadfast. Their camp stinks with sickness. Their food rots. Their numbers break. Allah is with those who endure."

The cry of Allahu akbar (God is the Greatest) thundered back, shaking walls that had held for three months. Ahmad prayed among them, forehead to stone, whispering: Oh Allah, give these people more patience than their enemies' cruelty. Give their enemies more fear than they can bear.

When the prayer ended, men did not scatter. A murmur spread instead—judgement had come.

The crowd surged toward the square. At its centre, soldiers stood in a ring. And on his knees, turban gone, face pale with sweat, knelt the thin-bearded scholar who had railed against Ahmad weeks before. His lips moved constantly, muttered verses, denials, bargains.

Abdullah, the amir of Arqa, stood tall before the people. His robe was patched, his eyes shadowed by long months of siege, but his voice carried iron.

"This man," Abdullah declared, "hid behind words while writing to the enemy. He promised them our gates. He spoke piety, but his hands drew maps for those who boil children in pots. Allah has exposed him. Today, Arqa delivers justice."

The crowd roared. "Traitor! Hypocrite!" A stone flew, striking his shoulder. Guards shoved the thrower back, but fury could not be hidden.

Abdullah raised his hand. Silence spread, heavy as an anvil. His gaze shifted to Ahmad.

"You uncovered him. Let your hand carry out the sentence."

All eyes turned. Some whispered relief, others nodded grim. Ahmad stepped forward, face carved from stone.

The scholar shrieked, "I did nothing! Only words! Better peace than blood! Why do you listen to him—a hunter, a savage?!"

Ahmad's eyes locked on him, hard and cold. His voice cut like steel.

"I have faced snakes with less venom than your tongue, in the name of Allah."

He drew the Damascus blade, sunlight flashing along its edge. The square fell silent.

With one clean stroke, the blade fell. The head rolled into dust. The body slumped forward.

A thunder broke. "Allahu akbar! Alhamdulillah! (All Praises belong to God)" Men shouted, women wept, children clutched fathers' sleeves.

Farid spat on the stones, voice sharp: "So ends a tongue that would have sold us."

Qays muttered, "Better one cut here than a thousand at the gate."

Sami's arms were crossed, but he nodded once: "It was just."

Nabil, quiet as ever, whispered, "May Allah protect us from more like him."

Abdullah stepped close to Ahmad, speaking so the people heard.

"You have done what fear could not. You cut out rot before it spread. May Allah strengthen your hand."

Days passed.

The city braced itself, but the storm never came. Scouts on the wall whispered that the enemy's fires burned thinner each night. Their songs faltered, their patrols grew slack. Sickness ate them faster than arrows.

On the fifth dawn, a horn sounded from their camp—long and thin, not of attack but retreat. Tents sagged, carts creaked, banners dipped. By midday their lines were breaking south, leaving only trampled earth and broken timber behind.

At first the people did not believe it. Then a boy on the wall cried, "They are leaving!" The words spread like fire through dry grass. From minaret to market, drums beat, voices cheered until the very stones shook.

Children ran barefoot through alleys, women embraced each other, gaunt men clapped each other's shoulders with the strength they still had. For once, Arqa's air smelled not of smoke and hunger but of joy.

Farid whooped and slapped Sami's back. "Even wolves couldn't drive them faster!"

Sami gave a thin smile. "Wolves can be patient. Their sickness did the work."

Qays leaned on his spear, muttering a prayer of thanks.

Nabil simply watched, eyes sharp, as if waiting for what came next.

Ahmad stood in the square, Nahhas bristling at the noise, Reeh circling overhead, Adham stamping the stones. He raised his hands: "Alhamdulillah."

But when the city roared, Ahmad stepped aside. He dropped to his knees in the dust, pressed his forehead to the ground in the prostration of thanks to Allah. "O Allah, You gave victory to your servants. Do not let us waste it."

When he rose, the city was still a storm of celebration. But Ahmad's eyes had already turned south.

That evening Abdullah called his men to council. A map lay open on the floor, stones holding its corners.

"The Franks march toward Tripoli, then beyond," Abdullah said. "There is little doubt—their aim is Bayt al-Maqdis (Jerusalem)."

The fighters exchanged grim looks. Ahmad's jaw tightened.

"They play with that city like dice on a table," he said. "But its people will bleed. If rulers will not stand for them, then we will."

Abdullah nodded once. "Then we stand together when the time comes. For now, rest. The road will call soon enough."

That night, while Arqa thundered with drums and praise, Ahmad stood alone on the eastern wall. The plain below was churned mud, broken shields, foul smoke drifting south.

"They go to Jerusalem," he murmured to his beasts. Adham stamped, Nahhas growled low, Reeh cried sharp above.

Ahmad lifted his hands, half-prayer, half-vow. "O Allah, strengthen the weak. Blind the hearts of those who would sell their own. Let me reach Jerusalem, and let me stand there until You decree the end."

Behind him, the city celebrated. Ahead, the road stretched south into fire.

EPIGRAPHS

"The Franks encamped before Arqa for three months, but God did not grant them victory. Hunger and pestilence afflicted them, and many perished. They took wood and food by force from the countryside, spreading fear among the villages."
— Ibn al-Athīr, al-Kāmil fī al-Tārīkh

"Our army was worn down before Arqa. The walls were strong, and the defenders courageous. Hunger and sickness pressed us sorely, and many of our knights and men died there."
— Raymond of Aguilers, Historia Francorum qui ceperunt Iherusalem

CHAPTER 17 — ALLAH WILLED THIS

The cheers in Arqa's lanes had not yet settled when Abdullah called the fighters to the courtyard. Dust clung to their boots, hunger still lived in their faces, but their eyes burned. Ahmad stood among them quietly with Reeh on his glove and Nahhas at his heel.

Abdullah's voice carried over the men.

"They march south, heavy with our grain. They think we will sit in our walls while they take the road to Jerusalem. Their path will have thorns. You will be them."

He pointed to a rough map scratched on a board with a blade.

"A convoy: carts, oxen, riders. Our people chained among them. And guides—men of our land. Strike where the track narrows. Break them. Free our kin. Bring back their supplies. And take prisoners. We will buy ours back with theirs."

His gaze fell on Ahmad.

"You fought for us on the wall. Fight with them now. Qays

commands, but your word has weight, and you are worth a hundred men. Qays, heed him."

Qays, nodded once. "He'll ride beside me."

Others were there too—men whose names had begun to bind themselves to Ahmad in Arqa's firelight. Farid, quick with a grin, still half in awe of Nahhas. Yusuf, young and hot-blooded, eager for battle yet always muttering du'a (supplications) before his blade rose. Bilal, steady and quiet, his bowstring always tight, words always few. Masud, older, with a cough in his chest but a hand as strong as any when the sword came out.

These were men who had laughed with Ahmad by the wall, who had listened to his counsel, and now would bleed with him on the open road.

They rode out east before noon, a tight column slipping through the gate into low hills of scrub and thorn. Arqa fell behind them. Ahead stretched land the Franks did not know, though every wadi and ridge was written in the fighters' bones.

By the third ridge, the scouts brought word. "Convoy ahead. Wagons, oxen, a handful of riders. Guides at the front. Our people in the middle, chained."

Qays marked the earth with his spear point. "Here. Archers on both shoulders. Riders wait until my hand falls. First volleys break their feet, second their hands. Riders strike the head. Ahmad?"

"Leave the tail open," Ahmad said. "Let them think they can run. When they turn, close it. Take prisoners."

He glanced at the men. "And if you see the guides smiling with them, you know what to do."

No one argued.

They split silent, archers sliding up the slopes, riders spread along the ridge. Ahmad sat Adham beside Qays, feeling the stallion's muscles coil like a bowstring. Reeh circled high. Nahhas shifted, eager, a growl pressed in his chest.

The convoy came: wheels groaning, oxen bawling, mail dull with dust. The prisoners stumbled in the middle, rope at their necks. Two guides walked before them, gesturing to the Frank at the head as if showing a guest the way to his own table.

Qays' hand rose. Then it cut down.

Arrows hissed. Men shouted, oxen surged sideways, the rope of captives jerked tight.

"Now!"

The ridge shook with the thunder of hooves as Muslim horse crashed down the slope.

A second volley fell ahead of them. A helm split. An enemy toppled from his saddle. The line bunched and faltered—exactly where Qays had wanted it.

Qays' lance took the first Frank under the ribs. Ahmad's spear shattered a shield, then he tore through the line with Adham like a black wave. To his left Farid whooped and drove his sword clean into a driver's chest. Yusuf's voice rose: "Allahu akbar!" as his arrow dropped a rider from his saddle. Bilal's bow hummed quick and cold, two shafts loosed in the time others loosed one. Masud rode low, coughing between strikes, his curved blade cutting an ox-rope so the beast tore carts sideways.

Steel rang. Men screamed. The ground filled with dust and fear.

Ahmad duelled a knight at the front, steel against steel, until Adham shoved the man's horse sideways. Ahmad slipped inside his guard and drove his Damascus sword up under the mail, leaving him folding into the dust with a grunt.

At the centre, the captives stumbled to their knees, choking on the rope. Ahmad cut them free with two clean strokes. "Run! To the ridge!" he barked. Two of Qays' men pulled them to safety.

The guides tried to back away, but fighters seized them, smashing one into a cart board and tying the other's wrists with his own staff. They would not be killed on the road—not yet.

It did not last long. By the time the dust settled, a dozen Franks lay dead, more wounded, six bound for exchange. The oxen were yoked again, carts righted. The ground stank of blood and broken wood.

But five men of Arqa lay still. One with an arrow in his neck, another trampled, another split by steel. Two more bled out before cloth and hands could hold them. Their brothers lowered them where they fell, not with the rites of the dead but as shuhada'a (martyrs).

Farid's grin was gone as he knelt by one. He whispered, "Do not call them dead. Allah says they live."
Yusuf wept openly and kissed his brother's hand before

laying the dirt over him.

Bilal tied a strip of cloth to a thorn above the graves, a marker for men, though he said, "They need no marker with Allah."

Masud spat blood from his cough and growled, "This land will carry their witness."

Ahmad helped lift the bodies into shallow graves, his hands firm, his jaw set. He did not pray the funeral prayer. He said only, "O Allah, accept them," and the men answered, "Amin."

They turned north with carts of grain and casks of oil, the prisoners roped, the guides bound apart. Dust rose behind them, a caravan of victory.

From the men behind came a voice, low at first: "Allah willed this."

Another answered: "Allahu akbar."

The chant spread until it rolled along the column like thunder. The Franks had their cry. Now Arqa's sons had theirs—not boast, but witness.

And Ahmad rode in silence, the hawk on his glove, the wolf below, the stallion steady under him, carrying both burden and vow.

CHAPTER 18 — CHOOSE THE PLACE

They chose a place where no one could hide. A flat stretch of hard ground lay between two low ridges, bare as a beaten plate. No scrub high enough to cover a man, no boulder big enough to anchor a trap. Ahmad had scouted three valleys and two wadis with the amir's riders before he agreed to this one. He pointed out the wind, the line of sight, the ways a man might lie and how the ground refused him.

"Here," he said at last. "If treachery comes, it won't come from the land."

The amir nodded. He was lean from the siege, his robe plain, his eyes sharp. "Then we set our terms," he said. "And we set our nets where we choose."

They wrote the rules on both tongues through a go-between: cloaks off at the approach, no helms, no swords, no knives, no hidden rods. Hostages to walk in the open, faces uncovered. Both sides to halt ten bow shots apart. Both sides to send an equal number forward—unarmed—to escort the captives across, one by one, at the same time. Any mounted man to stay outside the marked stones. Any breach would end the meeting.

"After," Ahmad said quietly to the amir, "they may still try to cut us off on the road."

"Then we prepare that road," the amir answered. "Choose the place."

Ahmad chose a narrow where the track bent around a spine of rock and dipped before climbing again. He put men on the heights with bows and wrapped their heads with dust-coloured cloth. He had picks open two shallow trenches and roof them with brush and dirt, stakes set inside at a slant. He scattered a sack of iron thorns—little four-point stars a blacksmith had hammered for him—across the smoothest line where hooves would want to run. Brush piles waited where a single spark would turn them to thick smoke. Light horse were set behind the ridge to swing left and bite a flank if called. None of it was grand. All of it was enough.

"Signals?" the amir asked.

Ahmad held up his fingers. "One hawk-cry for the volley. Two for horses."

The amir glanced at Reeh where she sat the glove. "Your bird speaks for us?"

"She speaks for the bowmen," Ahmad said. "Men will hear her faster than a horn."

The exchange day came grey with high haze. Both sides arrived in dust that rose and hung and did not fall. The Franks formed a line beyond the stones, banners limp. Ahmad saw faces he knew by type now—narrow

then broke; more men poured up from the hollow behind them—helmets back on, a scatter of horse in front, foot behind, a banner tipping as a captain urged speed. They had thought to cut the column on the rise where the road narrowed and the wagons could not move fast.

Ahmad did not shout. He lifted his hand and brought it down once.

Reeh screamed.

The first volley lifted and fell as if it had been one. Arrows hit men on the gallop before their horses knew why their riders moved strange. A mount went down screaming and tumbled its man into the iron thorns. Another slid into a trench, stakes took, and the horse's leg broke with a crack like a branch. Men cried out—language does not matter when pain takes it away. The charge bunched. More shafts fell. Smoke lifted up in the faces of the second rank as the brush piles took.

"Second!" Ahmad called, and did not need to.

Another volley dropped into the confusion, this one lower, angling for knees and flanks. Men stumbled into pits they could not see. The iron stars did small, mean work to soles. Horses learned fear in a single breath and taught it to the men behind them.

On the ridge behind them, Ahmad lifted his hand and cut it twice.

Reeh screamed again, twice.

The light horse swept off the left like a door being opened fast. They did not charge straight. They slid along the Frankish flank and bit at the soft parts—rear ranks, men trying to form, men trying to run. Spears took men at the hip, at the back of the knee, at the shoulder when a shield went the wrong way. A captain bellowed something that might have been "Hold!" and then an arrow took him in the cheek and he fell down.

On the road, the amir's main body did not bolt. They wheeled the first cart aside, made a living wall of men and wood, brought bows to hands, let the freed kneel behind the axles. A steady volley from that front kept the Franks from seeing anything but fear and pain.

Ahmad waited for a gap and rode Adham down three strides off the height with five men who knew his way. They did not press into the fray. They went to the edge of it and put iron into anyone who crawled out. One Frank in a mail shirt clawed up with a sword and a face black with dirt. Ahmad met his blade with a short sweep and put the point of his own in under the jaw and lifted. The man made a sound like a cork pulled from a bottle and flopped. Another came low. Ahmad brought the hook of his blade down on the wrist and felt bone. The hand fell off the hilt. The man made it three steps backward holding his blood and then a shaft from the ridge persuaded him to lie down.

It broke fast after that. A few threw down spears and ran hard. A few tried to drag wounded men from the pits and screamed when the stakes did their stubborn work. One group of six made a knot around a banner and tried to push it through the line. The amir's horse swung right and blocked them, and the banner fell.

"Enough," the amir said. He raised his hand and all along the ridge the bows lifted away from the strings. Smoke thinned. The sound lessened until only the animals' fear and the injured men's breath were left to fill the place.

"Take captives," he called. "Not many."

They took five who had enough life to walk and enough rank to trade. The two Arab guides were bound separately—marched with the Franks but not counted among them. Their fate would wait in Arqa, under questioning.

On the road, men lifted the brush from the traps and pulled the stakes and filled the holes in with their heels so no one would forget where their feet belonged and tear them open later. A boy with a jar of water went among the freed, telling them to sip, not swallow.

The amir rode to Ahmad at the edge of the smoke. His beard was grey with dirt now. "You were right," he said. It was not praise. It was a note in the record.

"They will try again," Ahmad said. "Somewhere else. With other men."

"Let them," the amir said, and nodded at the sacks and skins still in the carts.

Ahmad lifted his arm. Reeh dropped, talons finding leather, feathers warm under his hand. She clicked once, impatient. He smiled without showing it. "You worked," he told her softly.

They formed in order and moved. The ridge shadows lengthened. The smell of burnt brush thinned behind them and the smell of men took over again—sweat, leather, horse. The freed walked in the middle. One of the boys glanced back only once, at the ground where it had almost gone the other way.

No one on their side had fallen. It felt strange, almost wrong, after so many months of paying in blood for every small thing. Farid muttered, "I would have wished Allah to take me as a martyr today." Another young fighter answered him, "Perhaps next time."

Ahmad overheard and said, "Martyrdom comes when Allah writes it. Today He wrote for you to stay here, so fight. The day will come soon enough if Allah allows."

The men nodded, steadied by the words. They carried on, and the quiet said more than noise could have.

At the rise before Arqa's fields, the amir lifted his voice. "This is how we meet treachery," he said so the freed heard it and any man on the wind might carry it. "With readiness."

Ahmad spoke lower, to the men nearest him and to himself. "They'll learn. Every time they bend a promise, it carries consequence."

On the road behind them, the smoke from the broken charge drifted and flattened and went thin. Ahead, the city's thin towers cut the light. The carts rolled on. The freed did not look back again. They did not need to. The ground behind them had said enough.

CHAPTER 19 — BROKEN VILLAGES

The road south was scarred. Orchards hacked down for firewood. Wells fouled with ash. Fields crushed flat under hooves and wheels. Everywhere Ahmad looked, the land seemed tired, ground down by too many boots and too much death.

He reined Adham on a ridge above another ruined village. Smoke still curled thin from the houses, not fire but embers. Nahhas padded ahead, nose to the dirt. Reeh dropped to a splintered post, feathers settling with a soft rustle.

The village had been left in panic. Pots smashed, bread half-baked and abandoned in ovens. A man lay face-down in the dust with his hand stretched toward a doorway. Ahmad turned him over. The eyes were dry, the lips cracked — thirst had finished what steel began.

He moved on. A mule lay in its traces, throat cut for spite. Two women face-down, bracelets torn from raw wrists. A boy no older than eight slumped against a tree, skull broken. Another child stiff in a ditch.

Ahmad knelt and closed the boy's eyes. His own voice came rough, almost to himself:

"If they act like beasts, then let them see a true beast."

Nahhas sniffed the bodies but did not touch. Even the wolf knew shame.

From a ruined stable came the scrape of spades. Shapes emerged: gaunt men, women clutching children, a dozen in all. Survivors, faces hollow, eyes hard.

"Peace be upon you" one said.

"And peace be upon you," Ahmad answered.

At the words they came closer. The children flinched at the wolf, but Ahmad said nothing. Nahhas only sat, still and steady.

A boy stepped forward, voice thin. "Will you bury them all?"

Ahmad met his eyes. "Together we will."

The villagers set to work without another word. Boards pried from walls for levers, stones carried for markers. Ahmad dug with them, his hands black with soil. He carried a woman himself, laid her down gently, and covered her with earth. By the end, a row of mounds lined the edge of the field, each marked with a stone.

An old man looked at Ahmad. "You are the Father of Beasts."

Another muttered: "The hunter of Ma'arra."

Ahmad only said: "I am Ahmad."

Murmurs spread. Children crept closer. This time Reeh fluttered down from her post, landing on Ahmad's shoulder. She tilted her head, squeaking softly. Ahmad lifted her to a child's hand. The boy scratched her neck, wide-eyed. A girl touched her feathers with the gentleness of someone afraid of breaking them. Reeh sat still, eyes bright. Their laughter — thin, but real — broke the silence.

A woman came with a clay jar. "We have a little water. Take it."

Ahmad poured from his own skin into a bowl and handed it back. "Share this first. The children drink before I do."

Her lips trembled, but she obeyed.

One of the younger men burst out, raw with grief. "Where are the rulers? Do we wait forever?"

The silence that followed was not rebellion. It was despair.

Ahmad spoke flatly. "If you wait, hunger will bury you. The Franks are many, but they are men. They bleed. They fear. Teach your sons to throw stones, your daughters to carry water. Do not wait for crowns to save you."

No one argued. Some nodded, grim. The words cut true.

A boy asked, "Did your family die in Ma'arra?"

Ahmad's jaw tightened. He saw again the faces of boys lost there. He said quietly: "I was already an orphan long before."

The boy nodded, satisfied with that answer.

From a ruined pen came the bray of a donkey. Ahmad freed it, soothed it, and handed the rope to a villager. "Use it. Don't waste it."

The man nodded, speechless.

By evening the graves were marked with stones. Ahmad laid his palm on the nearest mound. "Allahumaghfir lahum warhamhum (O Allah, forgive them and have mercy on them)."

Then he mounted Adham, beasts at his side. From the ridge he looked back once. The row of stones caught the last light. Survivors huddled in the ruins, thin but still breathing. For now, that was enough.

He turned south. The road waited.

CHAPTER 20 — STRIKE THEIR HEARTS

That night, word reached Ahmad in the alleys of Arqa: Abdullah summoned him. He found the amir waiting with a handful of fighters — Qays, scarred and steady, Farid with his restless grin, Yusuf tight-jawed, and two younger men whose names Ahmad learned only then.

"The collaborators broke," Abdullah said flatly. "Their tongues spilled more than their letters. They gave us roads, convoys, camps where the Franks grow careless. We must strike before the host moves on." His gaze turned to Ahmad. "They have seen what you do. They ask to learn."

Qays spoke first. "We've watched from the walls. You make them believe shadows have teeth. Teach us. Let us do the same, so fear walks wider than one man."

Ahmad studied their faces, each drawn by hunger and fire. "Steel kills the body," he said at last. "But fear breaks whole armies. If you want to learn, then watch close tonight. At dawn you will not only strike their flesh — you will strike their hearts."

Plans were set quickly: the men would split into smaller bands, each to hunt a different track and spread terror in many places at once, lead by a few Ahmad had taught in Arqa. Farid and two others would ride with him first, to see with their own eyes how fear could be sharpened into a weapon.

In the dark of night spread across the hills in a pale, weak stillness. Mist clung low to the hollows, thick enough to blur shapes into figures and swallow sound.

Ahmad and the others prepared their clothes and faces to look like death, he lay flat on the ridge above a track, Farid crouched beside him, eyes wide. Behind them Adham stood black and still, breath steaming in the cold. Nahhas crept the slope below, ears flicking, and Reeh wheeled high as a dark mark against the paling sky.

The sound came before the sight: the groan of an axle, boots dragging in mud, oxen snorting against their yokes. Then the mist peeled enough to show them — a dozen Franks, armour stained with dirt, shields slung carelessly, helms at their sides. Two carts creaked with supplies. Behind them walked six prisoners: two women, one clutching a boy; an old man; another woman barefoot, moving like a sleepwalker.

Farid's hand twitched toward his sword. Ahmad pressed it down. "Wait," he whispered. "Fear works best when it surprises the heart, not only the flesh."

Then Ahmad strung his bow, exhaled, and loosed.

The first shaft punched through the throat of the lead guard. The man dropped without sound, spear clattering.

The second struck the soldier who had cuffed the old captive; he fell backward choking on blood.

The escort panicked, stumbling over one another, dragging at shields too late. Ahmad loosed again, another fell. The oxen bawled and the carts lurched.

"Now!" Ahmad snapped.

Nahhas burst from the brush in a blur, jaws closing on a soldier's leg. The man's scream split the mist. Reeh stooped and slashed the face of another who raised a horn; the horn gave one strangled blast and fell with him.

Then Adham thundered down the slope, Ahmad in the saddle, Farid and the others spurring close behind.

Ahmad's blade split the shoulder of the first man to bar his path. Farid struck another in the ribs with his spear, crying "Allahu akbar!" as the man toppled. The younger fighter darted to the prisoners, slashing ropes with shaking hands.

"Down!" Ahmad shouted. "Stay down!"

The captives dropped into the mud. The boy sobbed but obeyed.

The fight was chaos and mud and steel. Ahmad cut down a man at the collarbone; Nahhas dragged another screaming into the ditch; Reeh battered a third into blindness. The last two Franks bolted into the fog, shrieking. Ahmad let them go. "Fear runs faster than blades," he told Farid, loud enough for him to hear.

Then it was over.

The road was littered with corpses. The oxen bawled, the carts stood crooked, the mist hung heavy with blood.

The captives trembled, wrists raw. Ahmad pressed bread into a boy's hand and said to them, "Go east, into the hills. Hide. Keep yourselves alive."

When they were gone, Ahmad turned to the men with him. "Now you learn the part that matters."

He dragged one body to hang from a tree. Another he stretched across the track, the red cross torn so it looked seared into flesh. He poured wine across blood in the mud until the stench turned foul. He showed them how to smear paw-marks in the dirt, how to leave claw-rakes on wood.

"Make them believe the night itself hunts them," Ahmad said. "Kill one, then only he dies. Frighten ten, and a thousand will lose their sleep."

Farid grinned through the fog. "By Allah, they'll dream of this road until they choke on it."

Ahmad raised his blade to the throat of a wounded Frank still breathing. He did not kill him. Instead he leaned close, edge glinting. In broken Frankish he rasped: "Tell..., Demons... hunt you."

The man stumbled away sobbing into the mist.

Ahmad mounted again. Nahhas padded at his stirrup, Reeh leapt into the air. He looked once at Farid and the others. "Now you know. Go teach the rest. Spread the shadow wider than I can alone."

They nodded, fire in their faces.

The corpses, the freed captives, and the staged horror would speak louder than words. By nightfall, the Frankish host would whisper not of one hunter, but of demons walking in many shapes.

CHAPTER 21— I BRING FOOD

The morning was hard, Ahmad felt the tremor under Adham's skin before he heard the stallion's rough breath. Foam streaked the reins, sweat ran dark across the black coat, and the horse's neck worked as if lifting water from a deep well. Enough. Pushing him farther would break him.

He turned off the ruined road into an orchard that had once been neat as prayer rows. Now the channels were dry, branches brittle, and the air carried only dust. He slid from the saddle, ran a hand down Adham's shoulder, and felt the heat burning under the hide. He stripped the tack, lifted the damp pad, and let the air cool the horse's back.

"Rest," Ahmad murmured. Adham lowered his head and blew softly, grateful.

Nahhas circled once through the trees, ears flicking, then lay in the shade, eyes open but calm. Reeh rode the up drafts above them, a dark fleck against the pale sky.

Ahmad tethered Adham to a stump, loosened the girth another notch, and combed the sweat-dark mane.

His motions were steady, unhurried. When the horse's breathing eased, Ahmad slung his bow over his shoulder and walked the orchard's edge.

He remembered Abdullah's words before they parted ways outside Arqa:

"Go ahead of us. Take a smaller road. See what the villages became, and carry their voices back. We will follow the main track. We will meet again, further south."

So Ahmad rode alone for now — not abandoned, not severed — only a shadow thrown ahead of the column. He carried the same duty as the rest, only taken down another path.

The ground still carried stories. He knelt at a patch of soft earth and pressed two fingers to a footprint. Small toes, bare. Another, wider, turned outward. Not soldiers. Villagers. He stood, silent, and followed.

Smoke reached him before sight. A thin thread, fading in and out. He moved carefully until he found the source — a gully hidden by brush. A pot clinked. A child stifled a sob.

He didn't step forward at once. First, he hunted.

He set two snares from rawhide. A rabbit nosed into one, kicked twice, and stilled. Another followed. At his whistle, Reeh stooped, scattering two pigeons. Ahmad brought one down with a stone from his sling. Enough to feed more than himself.

When he returned to the orchard, he carried the rabbits and pigeon at his side in plain view. He wanted them to see him coming.

They emerged as the hungry always did: cautious, shoulders high, eyes hollow. Three women, two old men, and four children — one boy trying to stand taller than he was. Behind them, a crude burrow was hidden with brush.

"Peace, be upon you" Ahmad said.

Their voices answered together, soft, relieved. "And peace, be upon you."

An old man squinted, memory tugging at his face. "Father of Beasts," he whispered, almost afraid to say it louder.

Ahmad set the game down on a stone. "I bring food," he said simply.

One of the little girls stared at the wolf. Nahhas stayed still, muzzle on his paws. Only when Ahmad clicked his tongue did they dare move forward.

They built a fire no larger than two hands. Ahmad skinned the rabbits, salted the meat, and turned them slowly over the coals. Fat hissed, smoke rising thin and sharp. The pigeon he plucked fast, feathers scattering in the wind. Soon the smell of cooking filled the hollow.

He ate last, only a small strip. The best went to the children, then their mothers, then the old men. When one tried to give him some back, Ahmad shook his head. "Keep it. I've had enough."

Only when their hunger eased did the words come.

A woman glanced south. "Travellers say the Franks march toward Jerusalem. Their banners cover the plain."

The boy's voice came small but sharp. "Why are we alone?"

Ahmad set down his knife. "Allah is with us. Waiting for armies will not save you. We must fight. We must endure — not only with patience, but with strength."

The boy looked up, searching. "Strength?"

Ahmad nodded. "Do not wait for silk-robed men to decide your worth."

The boy's jaw set. The old man studied Ahmad with tired eyes. "And you? Where will you go?"

"I will meet my brothers again soon, we march towards Jerusalem," Ahmad said. "On different roads we bleed the enemy, and make them fear."

The boy straightened. "Then teach me," he said, ashamed of the eagerness in his voice.

Ahmad showed him: a snare for rabbits, a sling with stone, an arrow fletched with a steady hand. "The arrow will tell you when it is wrong," he said. "Listen." He whispered a Frankish word slowly: "Douleur." Pain. "Learn their tongue when you can. Words are another weapon."

Nearby, the little girl reached for Nahhas. Ahmad made a sound, and the wolf went still. She brushed his fur quickly, like touching fire. Then she laughed, thin but real. Another child was lifted onto Adham's back. Ahmad led the stallion in slow paces while the boy clung wide-eyed to the mane. For a moment, the orchard held something other than grief.

When the fire sank to coals, Ahmad checked his beasts: Adham's hooves and breath, Nahhas' teeth,

Reeh's feathers. Only then did he take a strip of meat for himself.

When someone began to thank him, Ahmad stopped them. "All praise is to Allah."

At dusk, Ahmad stood.

He slung his bow, mounted Adham, and gathered his beasts. From the ridge he looked back once. The living huddled among ruins, thin but unbroken. For now, that was enough.

Then he turned south, down the road where Qays and the others would meet soon enough.

EPIGRAPHS

"The Franks laid waste to the lands, burning villages, destroying crops, and carrying away the people. None who fell into their hands were spared."
—Ibn al-Qalānisi, *Chronicle of Damascus*

"They passed through the land like locusts, leaving nothing behind them, neither beast nor man, except desolation."
—Albert of Aachen, *Historia Ierosolimitana*

CHAPTER 22 — THE HUNTER'S PATIENCE

For three days Ahmad shadowed the army without ever meeting it.

He kept to the scrub and broken stone above the road, where thorn and oak clung stubbornly to the hills. Below, the rear of the Frankish host dragged itself south: carts groaning, oxen bawling, armour clanking against tired bodies. Behind the soldiers stretched the long tail of war—tinkers bent under tools, boys driving pack-asses with sticks, people carrying sacks, priests mumbling over beads on weary mules. When the wind shifted, the whole column stank of sweat, damp wool, and spoilt meat.

Ahmad did not fight. He watched. He listened.

At Ma'arra, their words had been only noise. Now he was learning their edges. He recognised the bark that meant "stop," the growl that meant "move." He caught their word for bread, their curse for broken wheels, their cry for wine. At dusk, he heard their priests chanting, each prayer ending with a word he already knew: Amen.

In his tongue, Amin. The world was wide, yet some sounds met in the middle.

He slept light, always near his bow and sword. Nahhas curled against his legs, warm and steady. Reeh roosted above, dark wings folded in the branches. When the Franks halted, Ahmad slipped past them through the brush. When they moved, he found another vantage point. He counted carts, guessed at rations, measured their pace by the distance a mule could cover in a day.

On the second evening he lay belly-down above a hollow where the rear guard rested. Men propped shields against spears, loosened straps, rubbed aching feet. Two quarrelled over a sack. Another sat with his face in his hands until a companion shoved food into them. A priest muttered prayers beside him. Ahmad could have ended them all with a few shafts. He did not. Fear would serve him better if he waited.

Near midnight he circled lower, keeping to the rocks. Nahhas ranged ahead, silent as shadow. Ahmad pressed his ear to the ground where carts had churned the earth, listening for the hollow echo of hooves on the track. The army moved like a beast—slow, hungry, careless. He meant to learn its every weakness.

On the third morning, he found proof enough. At a narrow pass where the road bent, wagons snarled together, oxen bawled, curses echoed. One boulder, he thought, could break their whole line. He tested a stone with his hands, felt its weight. Not tonight. Patience was the stronger weapon. The time for striking would come.

Instead he left signs. At a goat track leading toward the road he stacked three cairns, the way shepherds warned of danger. At a dry spring he scratched a mark into the rock: poisoned, keep away. At another he left a small cross of twigs—the kind scouts would understand as water near. Then he swept away his own trail until no one could follow. Hunters speak to the living without words.

That night he moved close enough to smell their cookfires. He watched men gnaw bread too hard for teeth, drink water gone foul, whisper of sickness in the camps. A hawk circling above them.

By dawn he turned his back on them, leaving the column to its misery. He carried their measure now—their pace, their hunger, their words, their weakness. When he rejoined his comrades, he would give them more than arrows. He would give them knowledge.

Reeh lifted from his arm and cut a line across the pale sky. Nahhas padded steady at his stirrup. Adham tossed his head, eager for the road ahead. Ahmad mounted and spoke low, more to himself than to beasts or men.

"Patience wins hunts. And this one has only just begun."

He rode into the folds of the hills to wait for his chance, a shadow trailing an army too large to see him, but never beyond his reach.

CHAPTER 23 — FIRE IN THE DARK

The host slept like a beast that twitched at every sound.

Ahmad watched from the scrub, counting fires, counting shadows. The camp sprawled across the low ground: wagons crooked, picket lines sagging, ditches filled with rain and waste. Hymns had dwindled to mutters. Sentries walked like men whose bodies no longer remembered rest.

He waited for the wind to shift. When the smoke rolled into the camp instead of out across the plain, he moved.

"Come," he said.

Nahhas slid beside him, a shadow with eyes. Reeh lifted from his glove and vanished into the night above. Adham stayed behind, quiet as an owl.

Ahmad carried twists of brush soaked in pitch. The first he tucked beneath baggage carts, where dry straw waited. The second he pushed under the oxen's ropes. The third he laid in a heap of thorn wood stacked for the morning's fires. He moved quick, unhurried, each step chosen.

Then the ropes. Pegs came loose under his knife. Hobbles fell away. Knots he cut half-through, so the least strain would finish them. A single free rope could do more than a dozen corpses.

Across the camp a sentry cuffed his drowsy mate. "Éveille-toi, ivrogne!" The man grumbled and spat.

The fires breathed.

First smoke, then flame. A shout rose: "Feu! Feu!" From another quarter: "Fuoco!" Fear braided their tongues together. Oxen bawled. A wagon lurched as its rope snapped. Men tumbled out of sleep, grasping for helms that weren't near, shouting for order that never came.

Ahmad was already at the prisoner carts. Sweat, sores, and rust. Five men sat shackled ankle to ankle. A guard dozed against a wheel, keys at his belt.

Nahhas was on him before he could wake, jaws clamped deep in his neck. Ahmad's knife slid under the ear to finish it clean. The keys rasped in the locks. One click, then another. The prisoners blinked into the firelight like men waking into a dream.

"Quiet," Ahmad said. "When I point, run. Into the trees."

Their eyes went to the wolf and the hawk's shadow cutting through the smoke. They nodded. One kissed the earth. Ahmad pressed the dead guard's knife into the youngest man's palm. "Cut the ropes."

The camp buckled. A mule tore free and dragged a rack of spears clattering into canvas. A priest ran with a cross raised high until smoke smothered his hymn. A captain bellowed for order, his voice cracking. A horn gave one strangled note before fire swallowed it.

"Now," Ahmad told them, and sent the captives running.

He fed the chaos as he left it.

Oxen stampeded blind, tearing lines, crushing tents. Wagons toppled. Canvas caught. Drums tried to answer but beat out of time, the rhythm of panic. A voice shouted diable! Another took it up. A camp full of men agreed on the name of what hunted them.

Ahmad left his marks. A ring of shields glowing like an eye. Claw-marks in ash. A cloak stretched high that twisted like wings. Each one small, but together they whispered louder than shouts.

He found one Frank crawling through the mud, blind with smoke. Ahmad hauled him close until the man felt the cold of the knife against his throat. In broken words the soldier would understand, Ahmad said:

"Run. Devil..."

The man stumbled away sobbing, fear carrying him faster than legs.

At the far edge of the camp, Ahmad freed one last prisoner, chained alone. No key fit, so he smashed the lock with stone until iron cracked. The man clutched at him in thanks, but Ahmad pushed him toward the dark. "Hurry. Quiet feet."

From the ridge he had started on, the camp looked like a city tearing itself apart. Fire flared, oxen screamed, wagons crashed, banners sagged. The great pavilion still stood, but its ropes sagged and its shadow bent.

Nahhas let out a deep howl to seal the mood, "Enough," Ahmad said.

Reeh stooped to his glove. Nahhas padded ahead. Adham came out of the scrub, ears flicking. Ahmad swung into the saddle calm as at prayer.

By dawn, he was a ridge away. The host below still shouted, still burned, still tried to believe order was possible. Ahmad watched until the sun caught the smoke and turned it into a haze.

They would argue forever about what had happened. Some would say a demon. Others would say a thief. But the ones with ash in their throats would speak truest: fear itself had walked into their camp.

Ahmad turned Adham's head toward the hills. His beasts followed. He left the Franks with their fires, their dead, and their stories.

Stories would do the rest.

CHAPTER 24 — THE WOLF
GETS A PACK

Night held the hills like a closed fist. No campfires below, no hymn or horn—only the breath of the wind through dry grass and the slow creak of branches. Ahmad lay on a shelf of rock above a dry ravine, watching the road's curve by starlight. Adham stood behind him, dark and still. Nahhas moved the rim of the ledge in a slow patrol, silent like. Reeh was a weightless shadow somewhere overhead.

He wasn't here to strike. He was here to wait.

A small clack came from the ravine—a stone tapped twice, then once. Not an animal. A signal, the kind men choose when they want to stay safe.

Ahmad slid down the slope with his bow in hand and the knife loose at his belt. Nahhas ranged a step ahead. Two figures rose from the scrub: lean men in patched travel cloaks, blades wrapped in cloth, eyes sharp from long miles.

"Peace," the first said softly.

"Peace," Ahmad answered.

The men looked past him to the wolf, then to the hawk's silhouette crossing the stars, then back to the man they had walked half a country to find.

"Are you Ahmad? We just came from Arqa, and before that Damascus," the first said. "Our ruler hides behind sealed doors. We will not wait for orders from a weak and lowly coward."

"Yes I am Ahmad, what are your names?" Ahmad said.

"Mahmud," the first replied—quick to smile, a bow-string-callus across three fingers. "And this is Musa." Musa's handshake was firm, his knuckles scarred, a strip of linen binding one forearm dark with old pitch.

"How did you find me?" Ahmad asked.

"Abdullah," Musa said. "We went to the amir in Arqa. He told us, 'Head south on the ridge and join Ahmad. If you're within ten miles of a black stallion and a wolf, you'll know him. The hawk will find you first.'" Musa's mouth twitched. "He was right."

Ahmad led them up to the shelf where Adham waited. The stallion snorted once, testing new scents; Ahmad's hand eased his neck. "Brothers," he told the horse. Nahhas circled, came close enough to scent their boots, then sat. That was acceptance enough.

Reeh slipped out of the darkness and landed—light as breath—on Ahmad's shoulder. She leaned forward and pecked at the leather binding of his hood, chattering in small clicks for attention. Mahmud stifled a laugh; Musa didn't bother to hide his.

"She does that when I speak too long," Ahmad said. He lifted a finger to scratch gently below her beak. Reeh's eyes softened, and she settled, content.

They ate without a fire: dates, a handful of nuts, a strip of dried meat. When the food was gone, Mahmud pulled a thin strap from his belt. "We didn't come to stand behind you," he said. "We came to stand with you. If we are to move south, teach us how you move."

Ahmad nodded once. "Then hear the rules."

He drew three short lines with a stick in the dust.

"First: no torches, no bragging, no steel unless it buys something more than noise. Men remember fear longer than wounds.

"Second: their possessions are our weapon. We cause a panic in their camp while they sleep. Loose one rope on a line of oxen in the right place and you can break a hundred men.

"Third: we leave marks for ours and none for theirs." He stacked two pebbles a hand's width apart. "Two stones at a water spot. Three in a line with one across—danger. A small cross scratched on a rock with two dots beside it means 'we were here; we left north.' You'll see shepherd signs like that. Use them. Change them when you move on."

Musa listened with his whole face.

"At night," Ahmad said, "you are what their fear needs you to be. You don't shout. You don't sing. You make sure the first man who wakes doesn't know what he's seeing. We dress dark and hide our faces in dirt, we place their crosses upside-down in places they shouldn't be. Shields set in a circle so the light makes an eye. Leave blood in their water and their food. Light fires to their tents while they sleep. Nahhas will howl when we are done so they cannot sleep soundly. Leave some men alive to run. They will do our work for us."

Mahmud's quick smile finally reached his eyes. "And if we have to fight?"

"Fight to end it fast," Ahmad said. "Knees and hands before necks. Take prisoners only when they pay for ours. Collaborators—" his jaw tightened, then eased. "—we hand to the amir. Information first. Judgement later."

Musa nodded. "Abdullah told us the same."

"We won't keep to you like shadows," Mahmud said. "Two men move quieter than four. If you'll have it, we split. You take us for two nights, show us your hand. Then we peel off and carry it to the others."

"What others?" Ahmad asked.

"Brothers of ours from Damascus," Musa said. "Three days behind us, maybe four. We told Abdullah where they'd pass. He said he'd send them down the ridge as well. We planned to meet again near the coast road north of Sidon—a village with a broken watchtower and two fig trees in front. We sent a mark there—a strip of red cloth under a stone."

"Then we're set," Mahmud said. He looked at Nahhas. "If I'm to learn, I should start with the hardest teacher." He eased a hand out, slow. The wolf watched him, pupils wide, ears delicate. Ahmad clicked his tongue once. Nahhas leaned forward and took Mahmud's knuckles in a warm breath, then turned his head away, bored with the ceremony.

Musa exhaled. "If my mother could see me now," he said, "she'd say I had finally found better company than the idle men at the mosque."

Reeh shuffled again, offended at the laughter, and hopped from Ahmad's shoulder to the top of his head as if claiming her proper perch. She made a string of soft noises that somehow sounded like scolding. Even Adham flicked an ear at that, as if amused. The men's low laughter died quickly back into watchfulness, but it stayed in their faces.

They settled the night's work without waste. Mahmud and Musa learned the hand signs—two fingers to the eyes for "look," palm pressed down for "low," Ahmad showed them how to wrap a knot to unroll with one pull. Musa practised until he could set it by touch alone. Mahmud learned Reeh's cry signals.

They talked of the road south only enough to agree. "We move again after moon set," Ahmad said. "We shadow the tail for one day more. No marks they can read. No bodies they can count."

"And then?" Musa asked.

"Then we go to meet the others," Ahmad said. "We'll learn how many backs we have. Jerusalem won't wait for us much longer."

"Jerusalem," Mahmud said, testing the word like a blade. "We'll reach your comrades before the city, if Allah allows."

"If Allah allows," Ahmad said. He didn't dress the words in anything else.

They set their guarding schedule: Musa first, Mahmud second, Ahmad third. No dramatics. Just a nod, a hand to a shoulder.

Reeh tucked her head under her wing. Nahhas curled where he could take first scent of anything climbing the slope. Adham shifted his weight and went to that heavy, half-doze that horses know when they trust the ground.

When it was his turn to rest, Ahmad lay back on the rock with his cloak over his shoulders and the bow within a hand's reach. The sky was clean and hard above him. He listened—not for hymns or horns, but for the breathing of men who had chosen to come. He had walked alone so long that the space beside him sounded different. Better.

Musa's low voice came from the edge of the ledge, a thought pushed into the night. "Even the best hunter needs a pack."

Ahmad didn't answer. He didn't need to. Reeh shifted once on his head like a crown made of feathers, and Nahhas exhaled through his nose, content. That was answer enough.

He slept, soundly and with beautiful dreams.

Before dawn they would break the ledge without a trace. They would move south along the ridge, three men and three beasts, with the road below and the work ahead.

The wolf had a pack now.

CHAPTER 25 — RIDERS INTO FIRE

The road south shimmered with heat, carrying the smell of ash long before the village came into view. From the ridge, Ahmad saw it first: roofs smoking, flames licking from one house, and the sound that stiffened every muscle in him — screams.

"They're in there," he said, eyes narrowing.

Musa leaned forward on his small chestnut mare, knuckles white on the reins. His beard was short, his face gaunt from travel, but his eyes burned like oil on water. "Then we ride. Enough watching."

Mahmud's hand went to the hilt of his curved blade, though he kept his seat steady on his heavier grey horse. His voice was lower, calm even in the fire's glow. "No wasted charges. We cut them fast, clean. Leave none to warn the rest."

Ahmad gave one sharp nod. "Follow my lead. Keep tight. Nahhas will close their backs."

The wolf's ears flicked as if he understood.

Adham surged when Ahmad loosened the reins. They thundered down the slope — three riders and the wolf beside them, earth shaking with their weight. Villagers were running in the street, chased by two Franks with spears. Behind them, another pair dragged a woman by her hair.

The Franks turned too late. Ahmad's spear struck the first in the chest, flinging him from his saddle. Adham crashed shoulder-first into the second, snapping wood and bone. The man hit the dust and did not rise.

Musa whooped a cry that was half laughter, half fury. He wheeled his mare so close to one Frank that his blade all but split the man's helm in two. Blood sprayed. "By Allah," Musa shouted, "they shall not escape justice!"

Mahmud came in slower but with brutal certainty. His sword swept low, cutting the legs from under a Frank who had turned to stab Musa. The man screamed once before Mahmud's second stroke ended it. "Patience," Mahmud muttered, wiping his blade on the man's surcoat. "Even wolves circle before the kill."

From the far side of the lane, two more Franks tried to flee toward the stables. Nahhas was waiting. He padded from the shadows, growl rolling deep in his chest. His eyes fixed on them, ears low. The men froze, their courage leaking out faster than their breath. The wolf walked toward them, slow, fierce, forcing them back into the open.

That hesitation cost them. Ahmad's arrow took one clean through the throat. The second bolted — straight into Musa's swing. His head rolled into the dust.

Silence fell but for a moment.

The villagers clung together, some bleeding, some wailing over bodies. Children peeked from doorways. Ahmad swung down from Adham and pulled the woman free from where she had been dragged, cutting her bonds. "You're safe," he told her. "Gather your families. Move to the orchards before more come."

An older man stumbled forward, clutching a staff. "Who are you?" he asked.

Before Ahmad could answer, Musa threw up his chin, still flushed with the fight. "He is Father of Beasts!" he shouted, proud as if the name were his own.

The villagers' eyes went wide, flicking from the wolf to the hawk overhead to Ahmad himself. Ahmad frowned but did not deny it.

Mahmud dismounted and knelt to help a child out of the rubble, his voice gentle. "Drink slow," he told the boy, pouring a little from his water skin. "Too fast will make you sick." Then, quieter to Ahmad: "These people have seen enough horror. They need mercy as much as steel."

Ahmad nodded once. "Then give them both."

Together they led the survivors into the cover of the groves. The men and women carried what little food was left, and the children clung to Nahhas' fur, the wolf huffed and let them stay, patient as stone.

When the work was done, Ahmad stood in the shade, dust streaking his arms. "You ride with me now," he said to Musa and Mahmud. "The road will be worse from here. But if you've chosen it—"

"We've chosen," Musa cut in hotly. "Better to die striking than a coward in bed."

Mahmud sheathed his blade with slow care. "Chosen, yes. We fight until Allah writes otherwise."

Ahmad smiled at them both. He glanced at Nahhas, who sat watching them as if judging his new pack.

Ahmad said quietly. "Then let us hunt."

They rode out together, three men, their horses, one wolf, and a hawk shadowing the sky. Behind them a village had been saved.

EPIGRAPHS

"They ate horses, donkeys, even dogs; some boiled leather from their shields, others grass from the roadside. Many died of thirst before they saw the Holy City."
— Fulcher of Chartres, Historia Hierosolymitana

"The Franks cried for water more than for bread; they suffered more from thirst than from wounds."
— Ibn al-Athīr, al-Kāmil fi'l-tārīkh

CHAPTER 26 — THE CONVOY

The night was thick and starless. The convoy crept along the stony track, torches sputtering in iron brackets. Between each patch of flame stretched only blackness — boots shuffling, wagon axles groaning, the dry clink of chains.

On the ridge above, Ahmad lay prone, still as the rock. At his side crouched Musa, eager hands tight on his spear. Mahmud knelt a pace behind, steady eyes fixed on the line below.

Adham waited farther up slope, stamping once, breath white in the cold. Nahhas slunk low to the ground, eyes burning. Reeh was a shadow even the night could not see.

Ahmad's voice was low, meant only for his companions.

"Twenty guards. Mail and leather. Weak discipline. They carry prisoners. That is our work tonight."

Musa's jaw tightened. "Then why wait? We can strike now."

"Patience," Ahmad said. His tone left no room for argument. "One breath too early and they scatter. We break them where the ground narrows. Watch, then follow."

He let the column crawl into the hollow of the track, where the ridge rose steep and torchlight failed. Then he rose to one knee, drew, and loosed.

The first arrow buried in — the man dropped without sound. The second struck the guard holding the prisoners' rope, his chest snapping backward, mouth full of blood. The line slackened. Captives gasped but froze, stunned.

The third arrow hissed into a horn-blower's hand just as he raised the instrument. He screamed, dropped it, and in that same instant Reeh stooped from above — wings hammering, talons raking. The horn clattered useless to the stones.

Nahhas launched like a shadow loosed from its chain. He hit a guard low, teeth crunching bone through leather. The man screamed as blood pumped hot into the dust. Adham thundered down the slope, a black wave of muscle and iron, scattering men before they even lowered their spears.

"Now!" Ahmad barked.

Musa and Mahmud went with him, sliding down the ridge in a rush of stones. Musa's spear skewered one man through the flank; he roared a cry of triumph, only for Ahmad's hand to shove him back.

"Quiet! The fear is louder than you," Ahmad snapped, then cut another guard from shoulder to spine.

Mahmud hauled at the prisoners' rope, cutting ropes with a captured blade, whispering for calm. "Steady, steady, you are free — move when he says, not before." His voice steadied the women clutching children, the old men who shook with terror.

The convoy dissolved into panic. A wagon tilted, spilling sacks across the track. Oxen bawled, dragged sideways. Men shouted "Diable! Jinn! Aux armes!" Fear braided their tongues into one cry.

Ahmad drove his sword into a man's chest, pulled it free, then pivoted to cut another's knee. Nahhas streaked past again, fangs flashing, leaving a trail of screams. Reeh swept low once more, scattering a knot of men who tried to regroup.

It was over in breaths. Corpses sprawled, wagons split, oxen bolted. Freed prisoners crouched in the dirt, shackles broken, eyes wide with disbelief.

He pressed food and water from the wrecked wagons into the captives' hands. "Go east. Hide in groves, caves, gullies. Help whoever you can."

They stumbled away, some weeping prayers, some too stunned to speak.

Together, the three of them swung into the saddle-lines and continued their march. They left the wreck behind them of fire and blood.

CHAPTER 27 — ANSWERING THE CALL

The hills grew drier as the host moved south, the air sharp with dust and thirst. Ahmad kept to the ridges, always one valley away, watching the Franks stretch out like a snake too long for its own skin. Their banners speared the wind — red crosses, lions, doves, and other marks painted bold.

He did not strike, tonight he searched for signs of his brothers.

They had agreed back at Arqa that if the fighters split, they would leave marks only they would know: three stones stacked under an olive tree, or a strip of cloth tied low on a thorn where no Frank would stoop to notice. Ahmad had watched for them every day. Tonight, at the edge of a dry stream bed, he found both.

"Come," he said to Musa and Mahmud.

Musa grinned, eyes bright even after days of hard riding. He was the youngest of the three, quick to laugh, and quicker still with his sling. "I told you they'd be here."

Mahmud shook his head.

Together they followed the signs until firelight glowed faint in the hollow of a ridge. There they found them: the fighters of Arqa, tired but alive, their cloaks greyed with dust, their spears still straight. They rose as Ahmad approached, and for a moment only silence spoke — the silence of men remembering the wall at Arqa, the charges broken, the dead buried under shallow stones. Then hands clasped forearms, shoulders pressed together, and words tumbled out after they greeted.

"You're still in this Dunya (World), Ahmad."

"And you too, Qays."

"By Allah, I thought you had beaten us to Paradise."

"No, not yet, maybe we shall go together, if Allah decrees."

They sat together under the rocks, sharing what each had carried. Ahmad told of the convoys broken, the captives freed, the fear planted in the Frankish ranks. The Arqa men spoke of their own raids, of food snatched from carts, of horses loosed into the night. Musa cracked a dry joke about Frankish oxen running faster than their riders, and for the first time in months, the men laughed loudly.

Bread was passed around, broken into rough halves. A skin of water went hand to hand. Mahmud kept his tone steady, always watchful, reminding them not to linger too long. Musa tried to teach a boy from Arqa how to load a sling stone faster. Nahhas padded through the circle like he belonged, while Reeh perched above, feathers dark against the stars.

When the talk grew quiet, Ahmad spoke again. His voice carried lower, but every man leaned in to hear.

"In the Quran, Allah reminds us: *And what is [the matter] with you that you fight not in the cause of Allah and [for] the oppressed among men, women and children who say, Our Lord, take us out of this city of oppressive people and appoint for us from Yourself a protector and appoint for us from Yourself a helper?*"

The words hung heavy in the night air, heavier than the arms on their shoulders.

Mahmud clenched his fist, his voice rough with conviction. "May Allah allow us to answer their call."

"Amin," the men answered together, strong as stone, the sound rolling through the hollow like a vow.

Ahmad rose, and the men rose with him. They formed a line, shoulder to shoulder, facing the direction of prayer. With dust at their feet, the sky above, and their supplications rising as one.

Together they prayed — hunters, farmers, orphans, men with scars and men with hope — bound not by names, but by the verse they had spoken and by the fight that lay ahead.

CHAPTER 28 — AMBUSH IN THE HEAT

The road south burned with dust and sun. The heat pressed down like a weight, turning sweat to salt and breath to rasp. Ahmad walked Adham part of the way, sparing the stallion's strength. Nahhas loped near the gullies, tongue dark, ears pricked. Above, Reeh wheeled, but even her wings drooped in the heavy air.

But Ahmad was not alone now.

Qays strode at his right, broad-shouldered, his bow always close at hand. Farid rode light, with the grin that made him seem younger than his scars. Yusuf kept to silence, his eyes sharp, every movement measured. Mahmud carried his spear across his lap, restless, as if he meant to strike shadows. Musa rode beside him, eager eyed, always too quick with questions and plans.

Six men in all, each hardened by Arqa, each bound to Ahmad now by the march, by the thirst, by the hunt.

They moved as one line across the land, their beasts among them, the dust of their steps rising into the heat.

By midday they saw them: a band of twenty Franks winding south, two wagons in tow, their shields slung careless, their step heavy. From the wagons came the smell of grain and skins of water taken from villages.

"They drink from our throats," Qays said bitterly.

"We'll take it back," Ahmad answered.

They gathered under a stand of thorn. Ahmad outlined the plan with swift cuts in the dust.

"Two men forward," he said. "Draw their eyes. The rest flank — from both sides. We strike when they give chase. No man leaves alive."

Mahmud spat into the dirt. "Let them run. We'll break their legs and leave them for the earth."

Farid grinned. "If I fall, Ahmad, you keep my wolf."

"You've no wolf," Qays shot back.

"Then let me borrow yours," Farid said, nodding at Nahhas. The grin widened. Even in heat and dust, the laughter was sharp as flint.

Yusuf only bent his head, stringing his bow. "Enough words. Let's move."

They moved.

Two men showed themselves — Musa and Mahmud — stepping bold into the open track, as if lost wanderers. The Franks jeered, cursed, and gave chase. Their boots pounded the dust, shields lifting.

That was when the trap closed.

From the scrub, Ahmad loosed the first shaft. It cut through a Frank and dropped him before his cry could sound. Yusuf's arrow struck the next, low in the thigh, spinning him down. Farid's shaft followed, straight into the chest of a captain raising his sword.

Then Nahhas leapt, a sudden snarl splitting the air. He hit the rear guard, teeth tearing into a knee. The man toppled screaming, his sword clattering away.

Adham thundered down the gully at Ahmad's whistle, hooves splitting the ground. The stallion smashed into the flank of the column, scattering shields like reeds. Ahmad swept low from the saddle, his blade catching one man across the face, another in the shoulder.

Qays came from the other side, his bow singing. Farid was at his shoulder, laughing between shots. Mahmud's spear struck a man full in the chest and drove him back into the dust. Musa followed with a cry, dragging a Frank from the wagon bench and finishing him with steel.

The fight lasted breaths. When the dust settled, bodies lay across the track, arrows buried deep, shields splintered, blood black on the hot stones.

One man crawled, dragging himself by his arms, his legs ruined. Ahmad watched him struggle, then nodded once. Yusuf's arrow whispered through the air and took him in the back. The body shuddered, then stilled. No one would carry tales back.

The wagons were theirs.

They broke open the barrels — grain, skins of water, dried meat. Qays muttered praise to Allah under his breath. Farid laughed and slapped Musa's shoulder. Mahmud drank deep and spat the taste of dust from his mouth. Even Yusuf allowed himself a thin smile.

That night they made a fire in the hollow of a ridge. They ate from the grain, drank water, and let the cool wind of evening wash the salt from their skin.

The laughter came soft at first — Mahmud mocking Farid's wild shot that struck a wagon instead of a man, Farid swearing it was on purpose to spill their wine. Musa joked that Nahhas fought harder than all of them, and Nahhas only yawned, muzzle red, as if to agree. Even Ahmad let himself smile, a brief thing hidden in the shadows.

Then silence fell, not from weariness, but from thought. The road ahead was short now.

"We are close," Qays said, eyes on the dark horizon.

"Soon we'll reach the walls if Allah allows," Ahmad answered.

The men stirred. The firelight caught their faces — scarred, burned, lined with dust, but alive. Brothers, not by blood, but by what they carried together.

Yusuf lifted his hands. "Then let us thank Allah for one more night together before the city."

They stood in the dust, shoulder to shoulder, six men and the beasts beside them, facing south. Their voices joined, low and steady, words rising into the dark.

When they finished, the silence was deep. Only the crackle of fire, the wind in thorn, the slow breath of the beasts.

Ahmad looked toward the horizon, where the road bent south. He thought of walls rising in the distance, of stones that would soon carry the weight of history.

"Tomorrow," he said.

The others answered as one: "Tomorrow."

CHAPTER 29 — THE WALLS OF THE HOLY CITY

The road turned upward until the land itself seemed to draw breath, and then they saw it.

Jerusalem.

The walls rose pale against the sun, the Dome glimmered beyond, and the air seemed thicker, as if the stones themselves carried centuries of prayer. The men reined in without speaking, dust rolling past their horses' legs. Even the wolf stilled, ears forward, as though he too felt the weight of the place.

"Subhan Allah (How perfect is Allah)," Qays breathed. His voice trembled.

Farid muttered, "Truly."

Everyone agreed.

They rode down into the outer streets. It was not what they expected. The markets were bare, shutters fastened, doors closed. Only hollow-eyed children peered out from alleys before vanishing again. No bells, no Latin priests, no open churches.

It was Yusuf who asked what all of them felt. "I see no Christians in the streets."

The answer came quick enough from an old man who leaned on a staff. "The governor sent many of them and the Latin clergy away. He thought it would spare him. But the old Christian families are still here. They will face what we face."

The men glanced at each other.

Silence pressed down. Ahmad said nothing. But in his chest a weight settled, heavier than his bowstring. He had smelled betrayal before; it carried the same stink.

Inside the walls, the truth grew clearer. Muslims, Jews, and the city's old Christians all prepared for what was coming. In the narrow lanes of the city, men carried stones to pile on rooftops. Women dragged jars of water into basements. Children hauled baskets of sand to douse fire when it came. Different creeds, same dread.

Most who stood the walls were Muslims, while Jews and the old Christian families guarded their quarters, preparing for fire and slaughter.

"They will kill us together," one Jewish man said flatly as Ahmad passed. His wife's eyes burned, fierce even in fear. "They will try," Ahmad said.

The governor showed his face in the square, flanked by guards. His words rang thin: promises of protection, talk of Fatimid reinforcements, hollow assurances that the city was strong. But even as he spoke, whispers spread that he had already packed his possessions, already planned his escape.

The Brotherhood gathered that night in the courtyard of a small mosque near the wall. The call to prayer rose, strong against the dark. Shoulder to shoulder, the men stood and prostrated, their voices joining with the city's weary defenders.

When the prayer ended, Ahmad lingered, eyes lifting to the great Dome lit by moonlight. "They think us weak," he said softly. "But we shall stand our ground and not relent."

Qays placed a hand on his shoulder. Farid grinned despite the shadows. Musa tightened the strap of his sword. Mahmud whispered, "Then let them come."

Above them the stars burned, cold and countless. Beneath them, the stones of Jerusalem held fast — for now.

EPIGRAPHS

"They encircled the city, building wooden towers and engines. Day and night they fought, but the walls held firm and the enemy rained fire and stones upon them."
— Fulcher of Chartres, Historia Hierosolymitana

"They besieged the city of Jerusalem and pressed it hard, cutting off food and water, while the defenders fought bravely from the walls and cast down upon them whatever they could."
— Ibn al-Qalānisī, Dhail Ta'rikh Dimashq

CHAPTER 30 — THE FIRST CLASHES

The first sun on the stones was cruel. From the northern battlements, Ahmad and his brothers looked out across the plain. Dust already hung in the air, rising from thousands of boots and hooves. The Enemy host stretched as far as sight — banners stabbing upward like a forest of spears. Beneath them, the men looked thin, burned, and ragged — yet they still marched. Hunger had not broken them, thirst had not detoured them.

Drums thudded, deep and steady. Horns brayed. The sound carried over the field and pressed against the wall, like waves beating on stone. The city shrank behind its defences, its people huddled in shadowed streets, whispering prayers.

Nahhas prowled at Ahmad's heels, lips twitching as if already tasting blood. Reeh circled wide, a black fleck in the glare. Adham stamped and tossed his mane behind the gatehouse, his dark eyes bright with nerves. The beasts felt the storm before the men did.

Beside Ahmad, Qays stood with his bow strung, arrows lined neat across the parapet as though the wall itself were his quiver. His face was still, hard, but Ahmad caught the way his fingers rolled over the shaft-ends like a prayer bead. Farid leaned forward, restless, his jaw working, eager as always to throw himself where the fight was thickest. Yusuf was silent as stone, lips set tight, eyes scanning every Frankish movement with a falcon's patience. Mahmud stood by the oil jars, steady as an anchor, waiting for Ahmad's word. Musa clutched his spear too tightly until Ahmad touched his arm.

"Breathe," Ahmad said, his voice calm.

Musa let out the air in his chest and nodded, shoulders loosening.

Below, the first Frankish test began.

It was no great assault — only a probing strike, a hundred men marching with ladders across their shoulders, shields lifted, and slaves dragging bundles of brushwood to choke the ditch. They thought to fill the gap with thorns and earth, to crawl closer step by step. Behind them priests raised crosses, their voices carrying broken Latin that Ahmad no longer needed to understand. The rhythm was enough: promise of victory, promise of heaven.

"Not yet," Ahmad told his brothers, as hands tightened on stone and wood. "Let them sweat. Let them hope. Then we cut it from them."

The men along the wall shifted. Rocks waited in heaps, spears leaned in racks, oil jars crouched under canvas.

The city's defenders muttered supplications under their breath.

The Franks reached the ditch. Brush fell into the pit. Slaves shoved bundles into the mud. Shields thumped forward. A ladder banged against a shield rim.

"Now," Ahmad said.

The sky darkened with stones.

Qays' arrow whistled through the slit of a helm and buried in an eye. The man fell backward screaming. Yusuf's shaft took another in the throat. Farid laughed loud as his stone smashed a ladder rung and hurled two Franks shrieking into the ditch below. Mahmud tipped a jar — oil rushed down, fire followed, brushwood shrieked as it lit. Flames leapt higher than the shields. Men wailed, rolling, their cries cutting even through the drumbeat.

Musa braced the first ladder to hook the wall. The wood shook with the weight of men climbing. His arms trembled — until Ahmad's blade hacked down and split the hands that reached. Blood sprayed. The climbers fell, the ladder flipped backward, and the crash crushed those behind.

"Push them!" Ahmad roared.

And the wall answered.

Stones fell like thunder, arrows whistled, fire poured. A spear caught one Frank through the ribs, lifted him, and dropped him into the ditch. Another ladder splintered under its own weight when too many men clambered up in haste.

Nahhas leapt onto the parapet with a growl that rattled the men nearest him. The first Frank's head appeared — the wolf met it, jaws clamping the man's face and dragging him sideways into the void. The scream cut off on stone. For a heartbeat the Muslim line stared in awe, then roared together, courage sparked alive by the beast.

The Franks faltered. A horn blared retreat. Ladders dropped, burning brush was abandoned, the ditch smoked with bodies and blackened wood.

The city's wall shook not from attack but from the voices that rose above it — "Allahu akbar! Allahu akbar!" The cry rolled down the battlements and back again, echoing against stone and heart alike.

When the last ladder fell, silence clung for a moment. Only the crackle of flame and the groans of the wounded reached upward.

Farid spat over the wall. "Is that all?"

Qays smiled thinly. "They'll come again."

"They'll bring towers," Mahmud said, voice flat, already thinking ahead.

"And rams," Yusuf added, eyes narrowing at the smoke.

Musa wiped blood from his spear, still trembling with youth and rage. "Then let them. We'll break those too."

Ahmad stood above the ditch, his shadow long across stone. He raised his voice — not shouting, but heavy, steady, enough to carry along the wall:

"Hold fast my brothers, Allah is witnessing our fight."

The men answered — some with cries, some by striking spear butts to stone until the sound was iron against iron. Together it rang like a promise.

Ahmad turned to his brothers. He saw their faces in the smoke and light — Qays steady, Yusuf grim, Farid fierce, Mahmud resolute, Musa eager and unbroken.

This battle was just starting.

CHAPTER 31 — SIEGE TOWERS AND RAMS

The siege engines moved like mountains on wheels. From the walls of Jerusalem, Ahmad and the Brotherhood watched the Franks drag their towers forward. Rope strained, oxen bellowed, men cursed in their tongue as the high frames rolled across the torn earth. Behind them came the battering rams, thick beams capped with iron, slung on chains to swing against the walls.

The defenders groaned at the sight, voices dropping into prayers and cries. Mothers clutched children behind the battlements. Dust rose with every turn of the wheels, so that the towers seemed to walk out of the haze like giants.

"In the Name of Allah," Ahmad said, steady, though his throat was dry. Around him stood Qays, Farid, Yusuf, Musa, Mahmud, and the rest — the men who had bled with him since Arqa, since the ambushes in the hills, since the road of dust and fire. Each carried a bow, a blade, a stone, whatever hand could hold.

The order was given. Arrows sang from the wall. Spears of flame arched through the air. Oil-pots smashed against wood and canvas. The first tower shuddered as its hide caught, smoke pouring upward. Men inside screamed, some leaping out only to fall broken below.

But the others rolled on.

"Closer," Qays muttered, drawing and loosing again. His shaft sank into the chest of a Frank at the ropes. Then another took his place.

Farid said. "They pull like oxen. Then let us be their butchers."

The ram slammed the outer gate with a sound like thunder. The stones shook under Ahmad's feet. Children screamed behind the lines. The men of the wall shouted louder to drown them out.

Ahmad notched, loosed, notched again, his rhythm unbroken. Beside him, Mahmud's jaw was set tight as iron, his face dark with smoke. Musa crouched low, directing others where to pour boiling oil, when to drop stones, his voice carrying steady even when the noise rose like a storm.

The tower pressed closer. Men behind its shield-wall lifted hooks, trying to seize the battlements. Nahhas snarled at Ahmad's side, teeth bared at the smell of them. Reeh stooped once, scattering a cluster of crossbowmen who tried to climb.

The tower struck the stone with a crash, bridges lowering. Franks surged up in a roar of steel. Ahmad's voice cut through it:

"Hold the wall! For Allah! For Paradise!"

The Brotherhood answered as one, their voices like a single body. Qays hurled a jar of fire, the flames catching a Frank's surcoat. Farid swung his sword down on a hand that gripped the parapet, severing fingers and sending the man howling into the press below. Yusuf braced a spear with two others and drove it through the first man who gained the ramp. Blood sprayed across the stones.

Musa pulled another pot of sand and ash, casting it into the faces of men climbing the ladder. They fell screaming, clawing their eyes, tumbling into the crush beneath. Mahmud struck the fallen with his blade before they could rise again.

Ahmad moved like the bowstring itself, loosing arrow after arrow into the tower's slits. When his quiver emptied, he cast the bow aside, drew his sword, and met the first Frank to set foot on the wall. Steel rang on steel. Sparks leapt. Ahmad twisted, slammed the man's helm against the parapet, and cut his throat clean.

The ram thundered again. The wall shook. Dust rained from the stones. Still they held. Still they fought. Still the Brotherhood stood shoulder to shoulder, each man a stone in the line.

By dusk the first tower was burning, its beams collapsing into itself. The second had been beaten back by fire and stones. The ram lay abandoned, its iron head cracked, its frame littered with corpses.

The Franks retreated at last, dragging their dead, their shouts bitter with rage. The walls of Jerusalem stood. Not broken. Not yet.

Ahmad leaned on his sword, chest heaving, smoke stinging his eyes. Around him the brothers gripped shoulders, bloodied but undefeated. Qays' grin was red with sweat and soot. Farid laughed once, sharp and wild. Mahmud whispered praises to Allah. Musa's eyes burned with the fire still in his veins.

And below, the enemy licked their wounds, readying for another day.

The sun bled itself into the horizon. The city still breathed.

CHAPTER 32 — THE HEART OF JERUSALEM

Inside the walls the city breathed differently: streets narrower, air cooler, shadows longer. But it was not the market or the houses that drew Ahmad and his brothers onward. It was the heart of the city. It was Masjid Al-Aqsa (Al-Aqsa Mosque).

They came to it as men come to a spring after days of thirst. The courtyard opened wide before them, paved with pale stone that held the fading warmth of the day. Olive and palm trees leaned at the edges, their leaves shaking in the wind. And there, at the centre, stood the mosque itself.

The dome was dark against the sky, the walls broad and steady. Arches ran along the facade, their curved stone softened by centuries of hands that had passed through. Lamps hung inside, throwing a warm glow that spilled out through the doors. Ahmad felt his chest tighten, here was beauty still standing.

They removed their sandals at the steps and entered. The coolness of the floor stones ran through Ahmad's skin like water. The hall stretched long and high, rows upon rows of arches drawing the eye forward to the pulpit, carved and tall, its place lit by lamps. The imam (prayer leader) stood waiting, a man with a combed beard and simple robe, his voice calm as if war itself could not shake it.

The brothers took their places. Ahmad stood shoulder to shoulder with Qays on his right and Farid on his left. Mahmud, Musa and Yusuf were also there, behind them came many other faces, known and unknown. Further yet stood the children of the city and behind them the women gathered in their own lines.

The imam raised his voice. "Allahu akbar."

The sound filled the mosque, echoing against every arch, rolling into every corner. They prayed and prostrated together, foreheads pressed to the stone where so many foreheads had pressed before. Ahmad's heart hammered in his chest. For once it was not rage that filled him, nor hunger, nor thirst. It was tranquillity — and the certainty that even if the walls fell tomorrow, the prayer they made tonight would rise higher than any banner.

When the imam recited from the Quran, the hall grew still. His voice rose and lingered on a verse that weighed on every heart:

"Indeed, Allah loves those who fight in His cause in a row as though they are a [single] structure joined firmly."

The words rang through the arches, firm and unshaken. Tears blurred Ahmad's vision and so too those beside him. The imam's voice slowed, letting the verse rest over them like a mantle.

The prayer continued, steady and sure. Prostrations bent every back, the floor cool beneath each forehead. It was not fear that drew their tears now, but love — for Allah and for each other. For a moment the city outside, with its hunger and war, did not exist. There was only light, stone, and calm.

Afterwards they sat together in small circles. Bread was shared, dates passed from hand to hand. Lamps flickered, shadows long against the pillars. Ahmad listened as his brothers murmured to one another — no boasts, no laughter too loud, only soft words of trust.

He looked again at the mosque, at its arches and lamps, its steady walls. Tonight the mosque was alive. Tonight they had prayed in the heart of Jerusalem, shoulder to shoulder, hearts lifted as one. And that was enough to bind them until the end.

CHAPTER 33 — A
BEAUTIFUL DREAM

The night before the end, Ahmad woke whilst laughing intensely from a beautiful dream, he had seen a glimpse of Paradise, it's rivers of honey, milk, water and wine. He saw the palaces and gardens made of gold and silver. He saw things that one could never imagine or even put into words and then he was told that he will enter very soon and that Allah is eager to speak with him, it was quick but it was real. He thought that he will tell his brothers when he sees them if Allah allows. Ahmad decided to stay awake and prepare what he could.

From the walls of Jerusalem the plain beyond was a forest of fire. Enemy campfires burned in lines, a ring of smoke and flame encircling the holy city. Hymns rose in rough voices, carried by the wind like a distant drumbeat. The words were foreign, but their intent was clear enough.

Inside the walls, the answer was softer. The call of Quran recited in courtyards, whispered supplications in crowded chambers, the thin voices of children repeating prayers they did not yet understand. The two sounds mixed in the air above the city, like a duel before a blade is drawn.

Ahmad now sat cross-legged in the dark of a stable alcove, a whetstone in one hand, his curved sword across his knees. Steel whispered with every pass. He did not hurry. A blade was not made sharper by haste. It was sharpened by patience.

Nahhas lay near his feet, tail flicking once with each scrape of stone. Reeh perched above on a beam, feathers tucked tight, head turning at every far-off noise. Adham stood saddled and waiting, stamping his hoof now and again, as if the stallion too knew that tomorrow would not be an ordinary day.

One by one the Brotherhood passed through the alcove. Qays checked his spearhead and muttered verses of courage under his breath. Farid spoke little, sitting with his back against the wall, feeding scraps of bread to Nahhas as though the beast were his own. Mahmud cleaned and re-bound his bowstring with the care of a craftsman. Musa laughed softly with Yusuf, sharing memories of Damascus that did not belong to this place, but kept the air human. They did not speak of dawn.

Ahmad told the others of how he woke laughing from his dream and what he had seen, Mahmud without hesitating said that he also had a similar dream the week before, the others said praise be to Allah, if Allah accepts our deeds, then they are true dreams. Qays mentioned that he doesn't remember his dreams and the rest said may Allah make their intentions pure for his sake.

A boy crept near the door, thin with hunger, his eyes too large for his face. He hesitated, then stepped into the gloom. "Hunter," he whispered. "Will we survive?"

Ahmad paused, looking at the boy. He saw in his face the same question asked in Ma'arra, in Arqa, in every place where children lived between walls and armies. He did not lie. "Allah knows best," he said. "But I will fight until I cannot."

The boy nodded once, as if that was enough. He slipped back into the shadows.

Later after everyone had left, an old man came carrying two dates in his palm. "Eat," the elder said. "Strength comes even from little."

Ahmad took one, split it with his thumb, and handed half back. "Together," he said. The man smiled faintly, and ate as if it were a feast.

On the walls, men shifted their weight from one aching foot to the other. They leaned on spears, whispered to each other, kept their eyes fixed on the dark fields below. Now and again a quarrel or stone would arc from the Enemy lines, clattering harmlessly against stone. The defenders answered with silence. They would need their strength when the ladders came.

Here and there Ahmad saw Jewish and Christian men as well, standing guard at their quarter's wall. Fewer in number, but no less determined. They gripped what weapons they had — axes, knives, even stones — eyes grim, their families huddled behind them. They had chosen to remain. Tonight, they were defenders of the same city.

Ahmad walked the parapets with the Brotherhood, bow over his shoulder, hand brushing the stones as he passed. He checked where oil had been stored, where spare arrows were stacked, where the weakest stretches of wall had been reinforced with timber. He spoke little. Once, when he saw a man's hand shaking too much to notch an arrow, he simply placed his own hand over it until it steadied. That was all.

The night deepened. In a courtyard, women gathered their children close, whispering prayers. A mother cradled a baby who had not stopped crying since the siege began. Ahmad passed by, and the child fell silent for a heartbeat, staring at the wolf at his heel. Nahhas lowered his head, sniffed once, then turned away, leaving the baby to its mother's arms. The women murmured to each other after Ahmad was gone, not sure whether to call him a jinn or a saviour.

Near midnight, the sounds of the enemy camp rose again — horns, drums, the clash of practice arms. Then a hymn, shouted in unison, so many voices that it shook the night. The words were strange, but the rhythm was of certainty. Men who meant to die made that sound.

Ahmad leaned on the parapet, eyes fixed on the shifting glow beyond the walls. He breathed slow, whispering supplications until the rhythm of it matched the beat of his heart.

A man beside him finally spoke, voice low and hoarse. "I am afraid."

Ahmad turned his head. "So am I."

The man blinked, surprised by the honesty. Ahmad added, "Fear is no shame. Shame is in running from the battle. Tomorrow, we stand. That is all we must do."

The soldier nodded his head and gripped his spear tighter.

The city breathed as one body — weary, thin, but still alive. Men slept in corners with weapons across their laps. Children curled beneath cloaks. A few laughed too loudly at nothing, desperate to prove they could.

Ahmad kept moving. He checked Adham's tack, adjusted the straps on his quiver, fed Nahhas scraps from the last of his dried meat. When he passed the mosque, he slipped inside. In the dark, only a handful remained at prayer, their foreheads pressed to cold stone, their voices cracked from fasting and fear. He joined them silently, bowing when they prostrated, rising when they rose, his own supplication unspoken but burning in his chest.

Outside, the night thinned. A pale stripe touched the horizon. The hymns of the Franks grew louder, more urgent, as though they too felt dawn drawing the sword closer.

On the wall, the captains roused their men. Buckles tightened, shields lifted. The muttering of Quran rose with the light, steady and sure.

Ahmad returned to his place in the shadows, sword sheathed, bow strung, beasts beside him, the Brotherhood around him. He did not speak. He only pressed his palm to the stone and whispered, "O Allah, if this is our last day, let it be one that makes you pleased."

The city held its breath.

CHAPTER 34 — THE BREACH

Dawn did not arrive so much as tear the night away. Trumpets split the air, and the north wall shuddered with the first full-bodied push.

Ladders rose like ribs out of the smoke. The tower creaked forward under its wet hides, higher than the parapet by the length of a man's arm. Rams boomed at the low gate farther down the curtain, blows in a steady rhythm that burrowed into bone. From beyond the ditch came the chant that had stalked their dreams for weeks—hard, ragged voices pushing one word like a battering ram:

"God wills it! God wills it!"

Ahmad was already on the wall-walk with the men he had come to know by their breath and their stubbornness. Qays stood two merlons down, calm as if counting grain, eyes always on the line, not the noise. Farid, the one who once joked he wished he too was Father of Beasts, heaved stones with a builder's ease, grinning through cracked lips. Yusuf kept the clay pots ready for the signal. Mahmud and Musa held spears with short grips. Two boys with slings lined small stones along the coping; a grey-bearded archer flexed his fingers without complaint, as if his hands were not bleeding.

Nahhas pressed to Ahmad's calf, the wolf quiet because Ahmad was quiet. Over the smoke, Reeh carved slow black circles in the hard white sky. In the courtyard behind, Adham stood saddled and hot, stamping his hooves.

"Stones here," Ahmad said, flat and even. "Boiling water there. Save the oil for timber and men together." He pointed once; men moved without argument. Fear liked orders.

The first ladder bit. Hooks clanged against crenels and slid, bit again. Hands in iron gloves groped for stone. Ahmad stepped in, took the haft of the hook across his forearm, rolled his hips, and pitched the ladder back. It went down, three men with it, their armour thudding the ditch like dropped pots. The second ladder reached with better luck. A face rose in a steel visor, breath loud; Ahmad's blade crossed the mouth of the helm and the man vanished as if the wall itself had decided it had no room for him.

Bolts thumped the parapet. One cracked past Ahmad's cheek and buried in the butcher's shoulder. The big man broke the shaft against the merlon and stayed where he was, teeth in his lip. Ahmad tipped his head once toward the stacked stones. The butcher nodded and heaved a block the size of a head into heads that passed below.

The tower ground closer, its bridge snuffling at the crenels like a beast testing a pen. The men beneath it shoved with poles, swearing in their own tongues, and their chant rolled through the smoke again.

"Now," Ahmad told the boys. Two clay pots sailed, rags tailing flame. One burst short; the other struck the cowhide, clung, and crawled. Boiling water followed in a long pour, low and ugly; men screamed under the hides as heat found eye-slits and seams and every lazy stitch. The dark skins steamed, then their bodies sank. The tower did not stop.

Sappers swung mattocks where the ditch had been choked by weeks of work. A ladder walked again, its feet finding a lip no sane man should trust. One Frank, braver than wise, tried to stand on the top rung and reach. Nahhas hit him the first instant his weight left the wood, teeth closing where thigh meets hip. The man pinwheeled backward into his own.

The bridge dropped.

It slapped stone two paces left of Ahmad with the sound of a door kicked in. Men surged across, shields up, swords low. Oil was coin; they met fire with water, stone, and iron. The first three Franks died fast, the fourth jammed his shield into the gap and lived long enough for the fifth to stab past him. The press thickened. Qays' voice carried without strain: "Back one pace." They stepped as one, heels finding the groove they had cut with their own boots these last weeks. The gap turned into a throat.

Ahmad fought the weight, not the men. He cut wrists and ankles, the ridge of a helm that rose too high, pressed his shoulder into shields to shift a man's line half a finger's breadth, which is as good as a hand when blades are close. A Frank stabbed low; Ahmad stepped inside, felt the small, soft place under the arm, and made the cut with no wasted talk. Another rose with a hook; Ahmad broke the hook with his forearm and shoved the man backward into the one behind him so that two men fell where one had meant to kill.

"Hold," someone shouted. It might have been a captain. It might have been the wall itself.

The bridge shook under its own dead. Men behind it shoved more men forward. A banner tipped in the smoke—white cross on old blood. The crowd around it made space as one; a slot opened; better armour came to the mouth of the bridge.

Behind the line, a runner hit the steps at a dead sprint. "The low gate!" he cried. "The rams—the hinges are breaking! They're through at the north—to Al-Aqsa!"

"Two more volleys!" Qays snapped. "Stones! Stones!"

Ahmad risked a glance down the wall. Far away, the ram's beat had changed; the note after each blow was no longer stone but something tired and old. When stone is ready to give, even men who have never built a wall can hear it. He looked at Qays. Qays answered with a single nod he had been withholding all morning.

"When it goes," Ahmad said, "we fall to the first fork. Not to the square. The fork bottlenecks. They come on the left, we kill them on the right."

"On your word," Qays said.

The gate screamed. Not like iron—like a thing with a throat.

The tower bridge heaved and jammed. A spear slid past Ahmad's thigh and punched into the butcher's belly. The big man sat down and stared at his hands as though they had betrayed him. Ahmad killed the spear man and stepped over the butcher's knees without breaking the line. Musa dragged the fallen man back by the collar one step at a time, praying softly, then let him down gently as if he were laying a child to sleep in a hot room.

"Leave him," Ahmad said. Musa's jaw clenched, but he obeyed.

The gate gave. The sound shuddered the wall under their feet. A second horn answered—a long, thin line of iron blown into triumph. The shout rose like flame:

"God wills it! God wills it!"

"They'll flood the lanes," Mahmud said.

"Then we drown them in alleys," Ahmad answered. He lifted his hand and chopped it down. "Now."

They broke clean. Men who had learned to fight beside him did not need to understand a map; they understood his way: deny the wide ground, choose the narrow, fight where the enemy can't move with ease. Qays and Mahmud peeled left with the spears and the boys. Musa took the wounded and the old archer. Farid and Yusuf snatched two slings and a coil of rope without being told. Ahmad ran the parapet three strides and dropped to the stair.

They hit the lane just as the first wave boiled off the ramp at the gate. Adham came from the courtyard like a storm in black, hooves striking sparks, the stallion's shoulder taking a shield and the man under it into a wall hard enough that the stone answered. Ahmad swung into the saddle as the horse came past, hands where they belonged by instinct. He didn't charge the open. He took the first narrow and made it a mouth with teeth.

"Block the right," he told Musa. "Jar of water—not oil—on the cloth. Smoke only." Musa's eyes lit, understanding. The jar hissed when it met the embers. In the choke of the alley, thick, choking steam did what men alone could not: it stole sight and made brave feet falter.

Families poured into the lane ahead—a spill of mothers with infants, boys pushing old men on handcarts, girls half-dragging their grandmothers by the elbows. Behind them, moving faster than any father could carry a child, came a hard rank of shields.

"Yusuf! Farid!" Ahmad pointed to the spill of bodies trying to force themselves into a door already full. "With me. Now."

They went without asking.

The first Frank in the lane screamed "God wills it!" and rushed his shield forward. Ahmad let the shield go by the first inch, then knocked the edge of it downward with the flat of his blade and stepped into the man's space where shields cannot cover. He cut once under the line and felt steel greet him. The second came in harder, Ahmad cut his knee and hand.

"Go!" he barked at the families. "Inside. Inside!"

A woman in a red headscarf clutched a baby so tight the child did not cry—only stared, open-mouthed. Yusuf took the boy from her with one hand while his other cut a spear tip aside. "He's fine," Yusuf told her, voice steady as a market day. "He's fine, sister. Move." He shoved the child back into her arms when the doorway opened and turned to face the next man without checking whether she made it through.

Farid fought like a man who had waited his whole life to be exactly here. He whipped a sling stone into a visor slit at a whisper's distance, stepped into the stagger, and drove a short knife into the armpit seam.

Farid breathed, and threw himself at the next.

The wave thickened. From the lane mouth, a horn's short bark told Ahmad a second line had found the alley's rear.

"Seal the back," Qays called from behind the smoke. "We have the fork!"

Ahmad pushed forward three steps to buy time. Nahhas went low and left, where Ahmad's eyes could not be. The wolf bit a man who tripped in the neck. A second Frank spun his spear, thrust for the wolf's ribs; the head scraped along Nahhas' flank, catching only hide, and stuck in a crack between stones. Farid smashed the trapped shaft with a stone, jerked the broken spear free, and stabbed the man in the throat with his own weapon.

"Good," Ahmad grunted.

They bought a dozen heartbeats. It was enough to pour two households through the door and drag a third up a stair and into a roof-garden. Musa pitched a broken table into the stair and jammed it there to hold back what it could.

Then the waves came again.

"God wills it!" the men at the mouth screamed, and this time it was a tide of men behind a wall of shields.

A child—eight at most—tripped in the path and went down. Yusuf saw him the same breath Ahmad did. "I have him," Yusuf said, and before an eyes blink, Yusuf dropped his shoulder, took the boy under his arm, and drove his own body into a shield to make space to turn.

A spear struck from his side. It had learned where to look for men who saved children.

Yusuf grunted as if someone had punched him in the ribs, not speared him through. His eyes flicked once to Ahmad, apologising for nothing, and he pushed the boy into the doorway with both hands. "Go."

The spear came out red when the man yanked it free. Yusuf sank to one knee where he had stood and did not reach for the wound because there was still a man in front of him and he had not finished with him. He cut the man in the shin. The man howled and fell. Yusuf smiled once, faint, then lay down like a man done with work.

"Yusuf!" Musa shouted, rage raw.

"Keep moving," Ahmad snapped, voice iron.

Nahhas darted through the gap, tore a man's calf, and vanished again before blades could find him.

The door behind them jammed on a jar. Farid turned without being told, kicked the pot to shards, and leaned his shoulder into the wood while the last of the family squeezed through. A woman hung back, fingers white around the arm of a girl who would not leave her doll. Farid snatched the doll, shoved it into the child's hands, and shoved the child into the stair. "Move," he told her. He stepped back to the line.

"Farid," Ahmad said without looking.

"Already here," Farid said, grinning like a fool.

A long axe rose over the shield-wall, falling for Mahmud's head. Farid caught the haft with both hands mid-swing. It crushed his fingers and changed nothing about where the blade was going, but it slowed it enough that Mahmud got an arm up and took it in meat instead of bone. Mahmud snarled and stabbed low, then used the stuck axe as a lever to knock the next man off his feet.

Farid laughed, a breathless sound. "I told you—"

The sword that killed him came from the flank, short and mean. It slipped between ribs where breath lives. Farid looked surprised, then relieved—like a joke had indeed finally landed. He reached for Nahhas without looking and found the wolf's ruff. "Good boy," he whispered, and the wolf, understanding, leaned into the hand for his final breath.

"Farid is down, Hold the line!"

They held. Because there was nowhere else for their feet to go.

"Back to the fork!" Qays called. "Now!"

Ahmad stepped back on the count he carried in his ribs. Three paces, fight, two paces, fight. When a Frank tried to step on the dead, Musa split his ankle with a lateral stab that left the man crawling and screaming, his face in the same dust he had meant to grind other faces into.

They reached the fork.

Ahmad told them, "To the left."

A crash from somewhere deeper in the quarter answered them: a door giving, women screaming, a child's high thin cry that makes wolves look for cover. They couldn't reach their cries, the distance grew colder.

A knot of Franks pushed through, shields high. Reeh stooped low and beat wings in a man's face; the hawk's talons scored skin and eye, and the man flung up his hands in blind panic and lost the line. Nahhas flowed through the gap and hamstrung the second. Qays stepped into the opening and put his spear under a jaw and lifted.

They held the fork through one push and then another. The dead filled the ground.

"Back again," Ahmad said, voice lower now.

They peeled away to where an alley opened into a small square that the city had used for water and bread before war. It had a low lip of stone and two narrow entries. Ahmad had chosen it days ago and hidden the thought in his teeth.

They made their wall of men and stone. Behind them, the square filled at once: a dozen women with children; three old men who should have been in courtyards asleep; a boy with a bandaged head praying out loud without rhythm or sense. Musa counted them without meaning to.

The first Franks into the square didn't expect a stand. They expected panicked backs. When men expecting backs meet faces, they stumble. Ahmad used the heartbeat the stumble gave. He stepped out and put a blade where a man breathes and stepped back into line.

"Left entry!" Qays snapped. "Three!"

"Right!" Musa answered. "Two!"

They fought with numbers and breaths now, not stories. Men fell. More came. Somewhere to the south a bell rang—a sound the city had not heard in months. The bell rang again and again.

"God wills it! God wills it!" came again, closer, harder. The voices had changed. Men who think a place is about to break sing that way.

They were not wrong.

A knot broke through the left entry and got under Mahmud's spear before he could recover the line. He took the first man with the butt of the shaft, the second with the point high in the chest. The third shouldered him aside and found, behind him, a woman holding a child and an old man. Farid would have been there—he would have filled the hole and laughed and thrown a stone in the third man's mouth. Farid was not. Musa was. He took the third man's blade in his forearm—meat and bone—because there was no time to move the right way. He bled but did not drop his spear. He jammed the point into the man's knee and shoved. The man went down. The old man kicked him in the face.

"Back," Qays said, and there wasn't room to back, but they found it.

A mother screamed. She did not stop. A Frank had her by the hair. He was trying to drag her away from the child she held. Yusuf would have gone to her. Yusuf was not there.

Ahmad went. He didn't shout. He didn't waste the breath. He went low, blade short in his hand, and cut the man's wrist. The hand opened. The woman staggered away. The Frank swore and lifted his sword with his left; Ahmad put the point through his throat and stepped away before the man had finished falling.

They were losing. They all knew.

Musa, pale with blood loss and grinning, coughed blood and said, "I smell the scent of Paradise."

The next wave came with priests behind it, crosses high, lips moving—words they believed gave their blades weight beyond iron. The front line pounded the shield-rims with their sword-pommels and made their chant the hammer on the anvil:

"God wills it! God wills it!"

A girl—no more than twelve—looked up at Ahmad from behind him. Her mouth tried to be brave. It failed. "Will we live?" she asked.

"Not in this world," Ahmad said, because the truth is sometimes the last strength a man can give. "But we will stand as long as we can."

She nodded once, as if he had handed her something precious.

The push broke the left entry. Mahmud took a blade that scrapped his ribs. He grunted once and stabbed the man who had given it to him through the eye without anger.

"Close," Qays said.

They closed. The square turned into a funnel of blood and breath.

At the far end of the lane, a woman was cornered. Three Franks cut her off. She tried to go left; there was no left. She tried to go right; there was iron. She sank to her knees because standing had nothing left to give her. One of the men lifted his sword, not fast, not slow—the way men do when they want to be sure they will not miss.

"Musa!" Ahmad said, and Musa was already moving, arm slit to the bone and still the spear in his hand quick and sure. He took the first man in the hip and shoved him sideways into the second. The third turned to meet him; Ahmad went past Musa on the other side and took the third from the blind angle. The woman crawled away and took shelter where she could.

A horn sounded from the north, then another from the west. Not warning. Not victory. Coordination. The ring was closing.

"Fall back to the cloth market!" Qays said. They pulled the survivors with them—down the lane where bolts of ruined cloth hung like flags of surrender that no invader accepted.

They reached the mouth of the market. The world there was red and moving. The market had been a forest of poles and shade once; now the poles leaned like broken spears and the shade was smoke. Bodies clogged the cross-street. A child sat in the middle of it, legs out, staring at a doll as if he had never seen it before. The child's mouth worked around a sound that did not come.

"Take him," Mahmud said. Musa did. He tucked the boy under his arm.

"Line here," Qays said, voice soft. "This is it for now."

For now.

They set their feet. Nahhas ranged the short space in front of them, low and close like a blade held ready. Reeh screamed once and kept her watch. Adham stamped behind, iron on stone, ears flicking to every cry.

The next wave came into view—a clean rank this time, shields matched, helmets bright even with ash.

They lifted their blades and their voices together.

"God wills it!"

Ahmad felt the line around him breathe in, bracing for the impact.

"Brothers," he said, not loud, so the words belonged only to them, "behind us are women and children. We do not break. If we fall, we fall forward."

"Forward," Qays said.

"Forward," Mahmud echoed, blood at his side and light in his eyes.

"Forward," Musa grinned.

They stepped.

The crash swallowed the rest.

They fought until arms trembled and steel felt like wood. They fought until the chant blurred into the sound of iron and breath. They fought until the poles of the market were hung with rags that were not cloth.

They held—only a little, only a while—but enough to pull another handful through a doorway, enough to teach the men who would kill them that even men who know they are going to die can ruin a morning.

When at last Qays put his hand to Ahmad's shoulder and squeezed—the signal for the next, last fallback—Ahmad nodded once. He looked at the faces around him and saw what he needed to carry into the end: men unashamed.

"Next square," he said. "One more wall."

They began to move, step by fighting step, toward the last knot of lanes where they would stand again. Behind them the cloth market filled with men who called upon God while doing things God would never bless. Ahead of them waited the place where an ending had been waiting since before they were born.

They did not look back.

They did not have to. The city's cries told them every-thing.

CHAPTER 35 — THE DEVIL'S ARMY

The city broke in too many places all at once. Horns called from three directions. The enemy's chants rolled through smoke and stone and the sound came so thick it felt like weight on the chest. Doors that had held for a month gave way like dried out branches in a storm. The wind pushed ash down the streets until the air itself burned.

Ahmad and what was left of his line fell back by body-lengths, not streets. Qays touched his shoulder when to move, Mahmud and Musa held the mouth of each turn with the short, ugly thrusts that bought more time than they cost blood. Behind them, women clutched babies that cried; old men stumbled with both hands on boys' shoulders.

Down one alley a door blew inward. Two men lunged into the dark and came out dragging a woman by the hair, a blade already up for the child under her arm. Mahmud ached to help but there were too many near them that also needed protection.

They could not be everywhere. That truth cut worse than iron.

At the next turn the flow from three lanes pushed into one. Bodies jammed. Swords found backs, not faces. Ahmad and Qays made a wedge with nothing but presence and steel. A boy stood on a doorstep and threw stones at men in mail until a soldier cuffed him down with a shield rim. Musa hooked the rim with his spear as the man raised it to strike again, yanked, and Mahmud put a short blade under the chin strap. The man sat like a puppet with its string cut. The boy crawled under his mother's cloak and made no sound at all.

They reached the rise to Al-Aqsa. The steps that had carried calm feet at prayer now filled with screams. The platform above rang with iron. Men roared "God wills it!" at every stroke, or because they had no other words left to make sense of their actions. The steps were slick. Near the top, someone had slipped and become one more thing others tripped over. Ahmad took the steps sideways, shoulder to the press, blade low to cut ankles, not chests. Ankles are how a rush stops.

On the great court, everything was wrong. Where there had been lines of men shoulder to shoulder prostrating, there were bodies in those same lines, and blood made the thin channels between stones run bright. A child lay on his stomach with his arms stretched forward, the side of his head dark where a boot had passed. The doors of the mosque were forced and iron clad men shoved through them as if the house of God were a storeroom they had been late to plunder. A priest lifted a cross at the threshold and shouted words to bless the steel that followed him inside to slaughter the innocent.

Ahmad felt the tremor run through the men around him—the same shudder that had run through their spines the first time the tower's bridge slapped stone. He didn't let the tremor settle. He pointed to the structure that ran along the eastern edge of the court—narrow pillars, choke points.

"There," he said. "We make a mouth. We do not give them open ground."

They ran. Behind them a knot of Jews and Christians tried to rally at the far side, backs to a wall, a dozen men with knives and two with bows, beards tangled with ash, eyes hard, guarding a press of families. Ahmad saw one bow bend, take a man in the throat as he stepped onto the platform. He saw the archer laugh once without sound and string again. Ahmad lifted his chin at him from across the court. The man tightened his mouth, nodded once. There was no space for more.

They set a last line in the structure: Qays in the middle, Mahmud to his right, Musa to his left, pale, left arm bound but spear steady, Ahmad in the front, two sling-boys behind the pillars with stones lined out in little rows and a grey-bearded archer with two arrows left. Nahhas ranged low and close, choosing gaps faster than men could name them. Reeh shrieked above the courtyard and stooped through smoke, not to kill, but to make men blink at the wrong time. Adham stamped behind the line, too big to fit the structure, too hot to stand still, rearing his hooves at every red-cross shield that came too near, sending them flying.

The first shove hit the pillars and split. The structure took the weight and gave it back wrong, sending men stumbling side-on into edges and stone. Ahmad cut where wrists show; Qays fought quiet, a pendulum of death; the old archer put a shaft through a visor slit and did not bother to watch the man fall; the boys' stones cracked teeth and stole eyes.

The press broke left. Three men slipped into the span between pillar and wall, blades low for the soft behind a shield. Mahmud met them with the butt of his spear under one chin, then the point into another's groin, then he missed the thrust that mattered because the third man had not come for him at all. He had come for the women behind.

"Mahmud!" Musa roared, but the warning was late by the width of a finger. The man's blade went past Mahmud's ribs and out his back. Mahmud took a step as if to continue, then turned once to face the sky and drew breath to make one final move. He drove his spear through the face of the man who had opened him. Then he sagged onto his knees like a man kneeling for prayer. Musa dragged Mahmud closer by his belt.

"Rest now my brother," Ahmad said.

Mahmud's smiled, and closed his eyes when he could not hold them open anymore.

A fresh wave came.

They broke the defenders. Not by strategy but by numbers.

The first man through made for Nahhas. He had been watching the wolf and wanted the glory of killing the thing that had pulled his friend down in the lane. He jabbed low. Nahhas darted. The second man had been waiting for the dart. His spear found ribs this time, iron driven to the bone. Nahhas' body jolted; he did not howl. He turned on the shaft, bit down on the second man's thigh and locked his jaw like a trap. The second man screamed and flailed. The first man kicked the wolf's belly to drive him off and could not. The third man planted a boot and pushed the spear deeper and the wolf's body shuddered. He did not let go until Ahmad's blade reached them.

Ahmad cut the spear's head off at the mouth of the wound and the iron inside Nahhas stopped moving. The wolf's jaw opened by inches, then stayed ajar. He slid forward until his head touched Ahmad's boot. His eyes found Ahmad's face and did not look away. He breathed once, shallow. A second time. Ahmad put his hand to the ruff and felt the last breath leave under his palm. Nahhas' body loosened, heavy at once. He had been with Ahmad since before any man had called him Father of Beasts. He lay with his face toward Ahmad and did not blink again.

There was no breath to grieve. The men who had put iron in the wolf lifted their shields and came on. Ahmad stood over his beast and cut men because there was no other thing to do that would honour the dead.

"Close!" Qays called, voice hoarse now.

They closed, and each time they did there were fewer of them to do the closing.

"God wills it!" the court roared. A cross tipped over the heads of men at a run, a priest under it sweating, eyes bright with a joy Ahmad did not understand.

The grey-bearded archer put his last arrow through the priest's throat at five paces. The cross wobbled, knocked the man to his knees, and then went flat into blood. The archer tossed the bow aside and took a knife from his belt. He stepped into the first man who came and put the knife into him three times fast, then took a blade across the face and fell backward without sound.

Adham screamed. Arrows found his flank, neck and rump all at once from men who had decided the horse was a demon they could kill. He reared and struck a man's head to pulp with both front hooves and turned so sharp his shoes struck sparks. A spear caught him high in the chest. He bit at the shaft like a stallion bites at a lead roped wrong and pushed forward against it until the man at the other end fell. Ahmad slapped the stallion's neck hard.

"Go!" he shouted. "Go!"

Adham tried to press his head into Ahmad's chest like a frightened child, blood stringing from his mouth. He could not go. There was nowhere to go. He swung across the court with blind rage charging through lines of enemies and trampling any who stood in front of him, then a wall of men closed around him and the last Ahmad saw of him, he fell down under overwhelming spears and swords.

"Back!" Qays shouted. "Back to the steps!"

They went because Qays had said it and because behind them, at the far side of the compound, a knot of women had been trapped against the platform edge where the paving ends and the drop begins. Men in mail walked towards them, cutting as they went. A girl stood with her back to a pillar, both hands up as if to hold back a sword, and the sword came down through both hands into her head.

There are moments when men become more than what they had been and moments when men learn they will never be more than what they are. The court held both kinds at once.

They made the steps. The steps became a funnel. The funnel became a place to die so others could go past. Mahmud was gone; Musa bled from two arms and a leg and still held his spear at the same right height again and again; Qays had a cut across the jaw that would have made a lesser man sit down and decide he had done enough for honour. He kept lifting and setting and thrusting. The sling-boys threw stones when they had them and, when they had none, they threw whatever they could because weight is weight when a man's face is close.

A column of men broke around the left. Ahmad saw them too late. He turned to meet them and something struck him from the side, hard and hot—an axe head with chips in it that caught the light for an instant as it passed. His ribs folded around the blade and then let it go. He stumbled and did not fall because the steps would not let him. He killed the man with the axe. Another came and he killed him too.

He looked over and saw Qays stagger. A blade had gone in low and up. He stepped once toward Ahmad, set his back to Ahmad's shoulder, and laughed through blood. "It seems," he said, "we stand."

"We stand," Ahmad said.

"Then stand," Qays said, still facing the men he hated, knife in his fist, until three men pounced over him and didn't let him stand again.

Musa took a blade in the throat. He made a noise unheard by most. He looked at Ahmad as if remembering something he had forgotten to say, then fell forward not to speak again.

For a breath there was a ring of space around Ahmad. The men outside it stopped as if they had run to a cliff and found the drop deeper than they had believed. He heard men panting. He heard someone reciting a prayer in Latin.

Ahmad looked at what was left of the brothers around him—Qays, Musa, Mahmud each bled on the stones near him.

He drew breath. There was one thing left to say. It was not for the men in front of him. It was for the Judge who sees the street as it is and not as any man tells it.

"O Allah, witness—" he said, voice rough with dust and blood. "We stood. We answered the call."

He stepped forward into the ring and swung. The first blade met his and lost. The second slipped past and found him. The third he met with his forearm and the iron kept going anyway. Blows came from three sides, then from four. He fell to his knees when his legs would not hold him. He kept his hands around the hilt until some man's boot kicked it out of his fingers.

He went forward onto the stones of Jerusalem, face to the ground he had chosen to die on, cheek in the blood of the those he had loved, the enemies he had killed and the innocent he could not save. The noise went far away. The light narrowed to a strip. He thought of the dream he had earlier and saw its truth ahead of him, he was yearning to meet Allah with his good deeds and longing for the never ending pleasures of Paradise.

He laughed as loud as a roar, then there was nothing.

The chant still ran across the mount—"God wills it!"—and feet went in and out of the house of God with mud and blood on them. The prayer lines were filled with bodies. The mats drank what they were given. The pillars threw long shadows across faces with open eyes.

By evening the land had a look to it that would cause tears and anger to echo through history. Someone dragged a cross up onto the mount and planted it like a flag. Smoke from houses below blew in gusts over the city.

On the ground where Ahmad lay with his brothers, men stepped around the heap because it was in the way. One Frank stumbled and cursed and kicked a dead foot aside. A child's doll lay in the dirt with no owner to picked it up.

Innocence was carved from the city, only the devil's army filled the Holy city.

CHAPTER 36 — THE HAWK ALONE

The city was dead, the bodies of the innocent no longer moved and those left standing carried dead hearts, void of any goodness, the closest friends of the devil.

Smoke rolled in slow coils above domes blackened with soot. Streets once filled with purity lay clogged with corpses. Blood seeped into the stones until they glistened black in the sun. The paths overflowed with filth. The stench of iron and flesh hung everywhere.

No voices rose. No prayers. No cries. Only the crackle of fires eating roofs and the clatter of boots searching for more to kill.

Over it all, one shape still wheeled.

Reeh circled with steady wings, her cry cutting across the silence like something misplaced, alive where nothing else remained. She passed over alleys where children lay stiff in their mothers' arms, over courtyards piled with men who had tried to hold the line — Muslims, Jews, and Christians alike, their blood mingled on the stones.

Over Al-Aqsa, its stones were slick and red where worshippers had once prostrated to Allah.

The Enemies looked up as she passed. Some muttered curses, some laughed, others spat. But none could silence her wings.

Her shadow slid across the broken domes. There was no hand to raise for her to land on, no glove, no Father of Beasts. The air was empty of all she had known.

The city's heart had stopped.

Reeh cried again, sharp, penetrating. The sound echoed against the walls and died without answer.

She climbed higher, as if distance could make sense of what the land had become. From above, Jerusalem looked less like a city of Heaven and became a city of Hell, its streets became rivers of blood, heavy with smoke and fire.

The hawk turned once more in the empty sky, circling without direction, as though searching for the one who would never return.

She did not know where to go.

And so she flew on, alone, over a city that no longer was.

EPIGRAPHS

"Piles of heads, hands, and feet were to be seen in the streets. Men rode in blood up to their bridles."
— William of Tyre, Historia rerum in partibus transmarinis gestarum

"Never have we heard of such a slaughter of people, nor of any nation that committed such acts. In Jerusalem they killed more than seventy thousand, among them imams, scholars, and men of devotion."
— Ibn al-Athīr, historian of Mosul (c. 1200)

CODA — THE ARMY OF ALLAH

The city did not stay silent forever. Eighty-eight years after the cries of 1099 had sunk into stone, another army stood before Jerusalem's gates. This time the banners bore the name of Allah. Salah al-Din Yusuf ibn Ayyub had broken the Frankish host at Hattin, and now he came to the city they had once drowned in blood.

The defenders waited for fire and vengeance. They remembered what their fathers' fathers had done, and filled the streets with dread, expecting knives in the dark and walls painted red once more.

But when the gates opened, no torches were lit. No massacre came. Captives were ransomed, not butchered. Families walked out alive, not carried on shields. The mosques were restored, the churches preserved, the streets left dry with dust instead of blood.

When asked why he spared them, Salah al-Din answered simply:
"We shall not treat them as they treated us."

Where the conquerors of 1099 had brought sin and slaughter, Salah al-Din answered with righteousness and mercy.

The stones of Jerusalem remembered both, and so do we.

EPIGRAPHS

"The people of Jerusalem came out in safety. Not a hair on their heads was harmed, not a coin taken unjustly."
— Imād ad-Dīn al-Isfahānī, al-Fath al-Qussi

"When Saladin had taken the city, he gave order that no man should be harmed, and he commanded that all should be led out in safety."
— Ernoul Chronicle

CLOSING AUTHOR'S NOTE

I write of the nameless who stood on those walls.

I write of their hunger, their fear, their endurance, though no chronicle preserved them.

I write of the cycle that has never ended — oath and betrayal, cruelty and mercy, truth and falsehood.

I write so that even in the darkest hours we may resist, we may endure, we may remember.

My words are only ink unless Allah allows them to stir hearts and to become action.

I leave you with the words of Allah:

"...and indeed, our return is to Allah, and indeed, the transgressors will be companions of the Fire.

And you will remember what I [now] say to you, and I entrust my affair to Allah. Indeed, Allah is Seeing of [His] servants."

— Quran 40:43-44

CLOSING DEDICATION

To Allah, Master of the Day of Recompense.
To the One who gives strength to the broken and remembers
the blood of the slain.
To the Judge whom no oppressor can flee, on the Day when jus-
tice will not be denied.

ABOUT THE AUTHOR

Salim Ibn Ahmad is a writer and media creator whose work is rooted in memory, endurance, and the power of stories. Through his publishing brand, SleepForm Studio, he creates books and media that immerse audiences in worlds both remembered and imagined.

Growing up in the West, he often saw the Crusades told through a narrow lens, where Arabs and Muslims were cast as faceless enemies and history bent to bias. That silence, and the way its echoes reach into today's conflicts, reminded him that history's wounds are never buried — only repeated.

The Father of Beasts, his first historical novel, was written to restore balance: to tell the story from the side that was demonised, without distortion or sugarcoating, and to let the forgotten stand in the place history denied them.

Find more of his work at:
www.sleepformstudio.com